REDNECK JOYRIDE

Ne'er-do-wells losers, misfits and a few nice folks

by
Darryl Halbrooks

Copyright © 2004 by Darryl Halbrooks

Published by: Instantpublisher.com
and UNIPRESS
92 Apache Rd
Westcliffe CO 81252

To order:
www.unipainter.com
or call
719-783-0506
859-623-6551
Printed in the United States of America 2004

ISBN 1-59196-462-8

for Bonnie

Contents

Acknowledgements

As always, my wife, Dr. Bonnie Plummer is a great help to me in all things. For the first 55 years of my life, punctuation has been a mystery to me. Thanks to some harsh but loving words from her, I think the next 55 will be more *punctual*.

Sincere appreciation also to my editor Jennifer Wheeler, whose biting, houmorous critiques I fear and dread. But in the end I'm always glad to have negotiated that deal with her.

Finally I want to thank my students and colleagues in the Eastern Kentucky University Department of Art and Design, especially my good friend Betsy Kurzinger who is one of the best critics I have ever known. These folks are kind enough to suffer through my readings of first drafts while they go about their daily activities.

Author's Notes

Ne're-do-wells, losers, misfits and a few nice folks.

The *normal* stories in this collection are in many ways a continuation of those in the first collection. The characters are flawed. They may actually *be* ne're-do-wells, losers and misfits but they probably don't realize it because their biggest flaw is that they are self-delusional.

When my *abnormal* stories are categorized as fantasy or science fiction, I usually object. I don't care for categorization in literature any more than in visual art.

In 1998, I was invited to Ecuador as a visual artist by the Kentucky-Ecuador Partners in the Americas. The Ecuadorian artists I met seemed very interested in my work but always wanted to know what genre it belonged to, because of, I suppose, a certain need to label and pigeonhole. I always claimed that, "It's contemporary art," an answer which, never seemed to satisfy.

I was recently shocked, to find in a national chain bookstore, two of my favorite authors, Kurt Vonnegut Jr. and the late (how I miss him) Douglas Adams, sharing shelf space in the science fiction section with novels illustrated by tacky paintings of big-breasted alien moon-women. Please!

To be mentioned in the same breath with witty, insightful, seriously scientifically minded, fantastically imaginative Douglas Adams would please me greatly. (Do you see what I mean about being self-delusional?)

But I suppose it's human nature to want to categorize, so well . . . go ahead if you must.

But—my creative license, a non-renewable permit issued by the Creative License Bureau in Indianapolis Indiana, sanctions me as a visual artist, to write about a world where dogs talk, parrots rob liquor stores, and former Indiana high school basketball teammates reunite with other classmates in a hellish New York underworld.

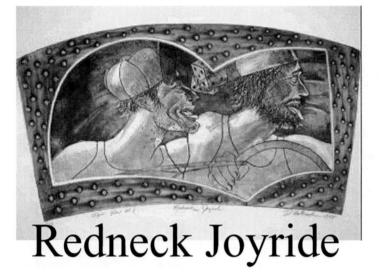

Redneck Joyride

CC Empty

Sometimes Clara wished she had paid more attention when Otto had tried to explain how the water heater worked—or what a pilot light did, or a carburetor, a fuel pump, a chain saw. Of course some of these things would only matter, she knew, if she had ever learned how to drive.

She admired Esther. After Henry passed away, Esther took driving lessons. But then she always was a go-getter. Now, Esther seemed happier than she had when Henry was alive. Said so too. Said she felt "independent" for the first time in her life.

To Clara, this independence wasn't all it was cracked up to be. True, she was getting by much better than she would ever have thought just a year ago. At least she knew how to balance the checkbook. Otto had never even tried to let her in on that mystery. Turned out, she had a real knack for figures. She actually looked forward to the first of each month when her social security check and the pension check from Otto's thirty-seven years at the gas and electric company came in. Esther had helped her set it up so that the money went straight into her account. *Direct Deposit* is what they call it. Even better than when she and Otto used to drive down to the bank and wait at the drive-through to deposit the checks.

And Esther had given her the cutest little red calculator—even showed her how to use it one morning over coffee and sweet rolls. It was translucent. Like a little jewel, she thought. She liked the way you could see into it. All its working parts were right in there, even if she didn't know which ones did the job of adding or subtracting all those numbers and spitting out answers on the little display. She actually looked forward to paying her bills. It wasn't just the competent feeling of knowing how to do it, how to use the calculator and write the figures in neat columns into the check register. She actually liked seeing the money disappear before her eyes. When she finished she knew exactly what was left for the rest of the month.

She sipped at her morning coffee. Thinking about recent changes in her life brought back the image of Otto—peaceful as could be in his Lazy-Boy, paper in his lap, kicked back, relaxed—dead as a doornail. She shook her head, trying to erase that memory. At that moment she heard two beeps of a car horn and went to peek out the living room window. It was Esther in her little red Japanese car. But this was Monday. Wednesday was the day she always came to take her to the Piggly Wiggly.

She opened the door and waved as Esther got out and walked up the drive. All dressed up—heels, patent leather purse, pink dress. She walked stiffly, sort of listing to one side like that old Life magazine picture of the Andrea Dorea. Must be the heels.

"What in the world?" Clara asked.

"Get dressed. We're goin' into town to see the queen."

"The queen. What queen? What are you talking about?"

"Queen's comin' to Lexington," Esther said. "Prince too, maybe. To Keeneland. Get dressed."

"Keeneland," Clara said. "But they're not running now. The meet was over more than a month ago."

But from Esther, no further explanation was forthcoming.

Well, Esther knew so much more about things than

she did. If a queen was coming and Esther wanted to see her, there it was.

"Can I get you some coffee while you wait? I have to shower and dress. It'll take me a few minutes."

"Coffee," Esther echoed absently. "Queen's comin'."

Esther walked, in her new stiff, tilted gait, over to the little breakfast nook and sat looking out the window. Clara watched her reach for the coffee cup placed in front of her and miss. Esther started to lift her empty hand toward her lips, then, seeming to realize that she had miscalculated, looked down at the cup. She stared at it for a few seconds, as though it were a moon rock. This time though, she lifted it successfully to her mouth.

"Are you feeling OK?" Clara asked.

"OK," Esther repeated.

When Clara appeared in the kitchen again, now all dolled up like her friend, she saw that the Esther's cup was still two thirds full and that the saucer and tabletop held the remaining third. Clara wiped up the spilled coffee and took the cup to the sink. She twirled around once displaying her new dress.

"Well, what'dya think?" she asked.

"Let's go," came Esther's response.

"Well," Clara said, "do you like it?"

"Looks good. Let's go."

Clara eyed Esther somewhat suspiciously as her friend pitched precariously down the driveway. Esther drove, faster than usual, out of the neighborhood and turned the car left, not the customary direction they would take to go to Lexington. Most people took the new road. But Clara didn't object. She liked to go for a ride now and then.

She thought about the drives she and Otto used to take on Sundays. Otto liked the old road.

"Can't see nothin' but cars, guardrails and Wal-Mart," Otto used to say about the new highway.

"Esther," Clara said, "I think you're driving kind of fast. Maybe you should slow down a bit." Clara was always reluctant to criticize anything that Esther did. After all, she was the woman of the world. But she *was* driving awfully fast and the car occasionally lurched and crossed the center-line.

Esther turned to look at her, not her head, but her whole body. The action reminded Clara of a puppet. Something else looked odd. One side of her face seemed soft, sort of melted, the corner of the mouth turned down. The other corner drew a straight line across her face in its usual disapproving grimace. With another robotic motion, Esther turned her attention back to the task of driving with the kind of determination that Clara imagined would describe Kyle Petty or Dale Jarrett Jr.— race-car drivers that Otto used to talk about.

They were out in the country now, passing cows and farmhouses at an increasing rate of speed.

"The Queen," Clara said, "trying to make small talk, "do you mean Queen Elizabeth?"

"Portabello," was Esther's inexplicable reply. "Portabello! Portabello!"

Clara did not want to upset her friend and decided not to press the issue. Who was Queen Portabello? She thought it might be wise to fasten her seat belt. She struggled with the apparatus. Usually she didn't like to wear them. She always had a hard time getting the clip pulled across her shoulder. Once that had been accomplished, she often tried unsuccessfully to get the thing clipped into its little buckle. Otto used to laugh at her because she sometimes managed to solve the puzzle just as they pulled into the parking lot at the PigglyWiggly. She felt a certain satisfaction now as she felt the snap, and looked up to see only oxygen outside the windshield. It was an odd sensation. Clearly, they had lifted off. They were flying. She had never been in an airplane. Otto had, but she hadn't. And now here she was—airborne.

When she awoke, she was sure she had been dreaming—something about flying. What time was it? She looked for the glow from the digital bedside clock but couldn't find it. She became aware of pain. It hurt to take a breath. She gave the pain a test, breathing deeply, but cut that effort quickly when the dull discomfort became abruptly sharp. She felt something heavy leaning on her left shoulder. She pushed painfully at the thing. It was soft—wet. Then she remembered Esther, the trip to see the Queen—Queen Portabello.

"Esther! Esther, are you all right?"

But she knew Esther was not all right. Suddenly she understood that Esther had not been all right—all day. She pushed her friend's body back into the driver's seat. It was dark, but from somewhere above the car, there was a faint light, maybe a glow from street-lights. But no, the light was too cool. It must be the moon. As her eyes adjusted she realized that she was covered in a fine powder and that a filmy envelope had collapsed across her new dress. The air-bag.

She reached down to unbuckle her seat belt. To her surprise, she accomplished this with great facility. She tried to open her door. A terrific pain shot through her wrist and the sudden intake of air from her gasp cause an equal pain to assault her ribcage for the second time. She settled herself and tried using her other hand to open the door. She learned quickly that she would have to do any heavy-duty lifting with her left. Still, the door would not budge.

She was surprised, when it dawned on her that she did not feel panic. She was not crying. Despite the desperation of the situation, she was in full control of her faculties and decided to carefully assess her

predicament—weigh her options. These were more or less,
the lessons of her calculator and her newly discovered
accounting skills. She would calmly subtract her debits
and compute her assets, weighing her options before trying
anything foolish.

She began with the balance sheet. On the positive
side of the ledger, she had assets: reasonably good
health—considering what she had just been
through—about 100 dollars in cash, a warm coat, a weath-
erproof environment, minus some cracks in the
widows—but as far as she could tell, none of the windows
was missing.

The car was not running. She reached over to turn
the key. Click. Ok. But—the car was not burning either.
What could she add to the equation? There was Esther's
coat, purse, money, cigarettes,—*lighter*. She, Clara, had
never smoked. She had always tip-toed around the subject
with Esther. Even after Esther developed that nasty cough.

"I just don't know where this cough has come
from," Esther had complained. "Just out of nowhere. And I
don't feel good. No energy."

"Have you ever noticed," Clara had ventured,
"They put those little warning labels on those cigarette
packs? Says right here," she picked up Esther's pack and
read from the label. "May be harmful to your health."

She had started to read further, when Esther
snatched the pack away from her with a look that said,
"I've read it."

She checked the glove compartment. Condiment
packets: ketchup, salt, pepper, napkins, car registration. No
flashlight.

Now the liabilities: Esther, her friend and mentor,
was dead. Not only was she dead, she was blocking her
access to the other door. Her own door, she could tell in
the dim moonlight, could never be opened, as it was
jammed against a tree. It was getting cold. She could not

rely on the car's engine to provide heat. No one would be looking for two old ladies who lived alone, not for days anyway. Her head hurt. She felt the knot with her good hand. How long had she been here already? It had been light when they had taken flight. Injuries: cracked rib or ribs? Broken or badly sprained wrist? And now a slow burning was beginning in her right ankle. She tried to reach across her stiff friend to the opposite door handle but it was too much for her right now.

OK Time to hit the = button. Result: Get some sleep until daylight.

She still had her coat on. She was able to reach into the back seat and pull Esther's coat up. She covered herself with both coats. It was odd. She felt relatively calm . . . happy even. But there was one more thing.

She had to pee.

"What the hell?" she said through shivering teeth, and felt a pleasantly warm stream of relief run down her legs.

During the long night, she drifted in and out of consciousness. It seemed that morning would never come. What if it did? During her entire life, nights had been the hardest—like when she was sick, or when her mother was dying—or the night Otto died. Morning had always seemed to provide some answers, present options. It occurred to her during one of these wakeful periods that she was an optimist. Her mother and sister had been pessimists. Even Esther, always seemed to predict a worst-case-scenario for every situation. Of all these folks, look who was still kicking. After this appraisal she fell into a deep sleep.

She awoke to another surprise. It had to be daylight that greeted her, but she couldn't make out anything outside the cracked windshield or the window next to her face. Snow. Several inches had covered the car, allowing only a glacial blue to filter into the interior. But beyond

Esther's gaping mouth, the glass on the other side of the car was clear. It was time to take some action.

Her injuries had stiffened and a determined and painful effort was required to unlatch Esther's door. She did not have enough leverage from her position to push the door open with her arm. Finally, she managed to extricate herself from her seating position and brace her back against the door. Using her good leg, she pushed Esther's body against the opposite door and her friend wedged the door open for her—still of service, even in death.

After a long and agonizing struggle, both Esther and Clara were free of the vehicle. Clara pulled Esther's body a few feet from the car. Clara's high heels were certainly of little use in the snow. The useless spikes pierced the three inches of snow and stuck suckingly into the mud below it. She heard a familiar sound. It was a car.

"Help! Help me please. Down here!"

They were in a ravine. The road, according to the roar of the car that went by, was just above, but about 15 steep feet above. She tested her ankle. Sharp pain. Useless. Her feet were getting very cold and wet. She apologized to Esther and climbed back in.

During the remainder of the day she heard several cars pass tantalizingly close by. This was ironic. Salvation . . . for Clara at least, was only a matter of feet away, yet she could think of nothing to do. After a meal of ketchup and snowball, she slept.

When she awoke the next time it was dark again. She had squandered the daylight hours in indecision and stupidity. There must be something she could do. Then she heard a sound that she could scarcely identify. When she did identify it she could scarcely believe it. A telephone. Yes. She remembered now, Esther explaining to her about cellular phones. How she might get one for emergencies. Clara had thought the idea was silly. The ringing was coming from Esther's purse. She found the source and pulled it out. She flipped open the little mouthpiece.

"Hello," she shouted, "Hello, Hello."

The little device kept ringing. She began frantically pressing buttons, shouting "help me." At last she must have hit the right button because she heard connecting sounds.

Did she wish to change from her current service to AT and T wireless?

"Help me please. I've been in a wreck. My friend is dead."

The voice answered. She felt an immediate and overwhelming sense of gratitude.

"You have received this recorded message in response to your application for wireless service in this area. If you do not wish to receive further offers you may contact . . . the voice faded and cut off.

Static.

She tried pressing a few more buttons but had no idea which ones were correct.

"Think this out," she told herself.

More calmly now, she worked out the button that turned the thing off and on. Oddly enough, the *off* button performed both functions. Sometimes there were messages. The message "CC empty" always seemed to bring an end to any attempt.

If she waited too long deciding what to do next, the lighted display went out. Then she could not see which button to depress next or what message she had been studying, because pushing the next button brought the lighted display back but deleted the previous message, presenting her instead, with a number or a new and equally cryptic memo, often culminating with the dreaded "CC empty." She did know something about batteries and came to the conclusion that the lighted display, as well as wildly punching buttons to get random messages, could render the little communicator even more useless than it had so far proven to be. She decided to turn in for the night.

The next morning she depressed the off button for just the amount of time necessary to turn the thing on. If she held it a second beyond that, she had discovered, she got "CC empty." So far so good. She read the display, which welcomed her. Now a vertical bar appeared, then two. She was not sure what this meant, but it seemed to be the best news the little phone had given her to date. She dialed in a number she knew well: 911.

She listened but there was nothing. She examined the display. That must be it. *Send.*

This time there was a connection and she heard a voice.

"911 operator."

"Help me, I've been . . . " She went through her explanation. She listened. Nothing. She examined the display. The little bars disappeared, followed by a new message, one she had not previously seen. "No service." Then another. "Battery low." Now a beep. The thing was as dead as her stiffened old friend out there in the snow.

After crying, for the first time since the crash—out of frustration born of the age of technology rather than as a result of feeling sorry for herself—she devised a plan based on man's first instincts.

Fire.

She had Esther's lighter. She burned every scrap of paper she could come up with to try to make a smoke signal. Any wood in the area was too wet to burn. In the end she burned the money, chuckling to herself because she started with ones, then fives then tens and so on. What difference did it make? The smoke of a one was equal to the smoke of a twenty. And wouldn't you know it? Esther had two hundreds on her. In this situation she would trade the two hundreds for twenty ones. A pretty good deal.

That night it was colder. She was hungry and thirsty. Her feet were in bad shape from repeatedly dragging herself out into the snow. She had managed to dig a little latrine. Even if she died here in the car, she had no intention of expiring in her own poop. Two days ago she might still have crawled and pulled herself to the road using her good foot and her good hand. But she had had some hope that a passer-by would have noticed the broken guard-rail and the snapped saplings that marked the trajectory of their car. But now she was weak and had only bad feet and bad hands. It would be easy. She could just go to sleep and stay asleep.

She went to sleep.

What was that noise?

She was dreaming when the sound penetrated the dream. It was loud. She wanted it to stop. She woke up and it did stop. She understood, with her hazy, malnourished mind that the sound had stopped when she pulled her head back from the steering wheel. Then she noticed something else. The little light in the open glove box was flickering off and on. She banged on the dash with her left fist and the light glowed steadily. Something that had shorted it out must have shifted or unstuck itself or melted. Something. She pushed on the steering wheel and the noise sounded out again. The horn was working. She listened for the familiar approach of the occasional vehicle. Each time she heard the noise building, she began blowing the horn rhythmically until at last she heard astonished voices above her, heard sliding and scrambling and branches cracking.

She lit up one of Esther's cigarettes and took the first puff of her life.

Blind Date

It wasn't that she was ugly or anything like that. Quite the opposite. The thing was, I guess the online dating service matched us up because we both expressed interest in art. But I didn't know she would actually *be* an artist. You know, dress like they do, act like they do. I just meant that I liked to go to museums, galleries. Like—Monet, Van Gogh—that kind of thing.

She picked the movie. Some art-house thing. *Bicycle Thief*. I didn't care for it. I'm not much on foreign films. She's sizes me up over her scotch, straight up—her second

"I actually have an Aunt Bea," I tell her. "She even makes pies and cookies."

Roxanne—that's her name, Roxanne. She narrows her eyes at me through the stream of smoke she has just released, takes another sip.

How would you picture a Roxanne, who says in her advertisement that she likes art, music—classical and jazz and runs thirty miles a week?

"Yeah, Aunt Bea was . . .is . . .great. She's always the one that the rest of us would hate to disappoint. She practically raised me."

The spiky, matte-black knife-blades of her hair threaten me, springing forward as they do from her forehead. "Who gives a fuck?" she says.

Now I don't know how you feel, but I always find this to be somewhat of a conversation stopper.

"In your ad," she says, the shiny stud in her tongue flashing between syllables, "you claim to be an art-lover."

It takes me a minute to compose my answer. I'm still hypnotized by the movements of the shimmering ball dancing around the dark recesses of her mouth.

"Well, I didn't actually say I was an art lover. I said I was interested in art. You know. I wanted to seem interesting."

"You are interesting," She says. "You're as interesting as all the others."

"All the others?"

"Yeah," she blows smoke at me and leans in, resting her chin on her palm. She sticks her tongue out and lets it curl forward, exposing the stud she knows I have not been able to take my eyes from. She pulls it back in with a waving motion that reads as a kind of taunting invitation.

"You're like them of course. Except you're less secure and you come from what *you* think is a more interesting family background. Aunt Bea, and Sheriff Taylor and Thelma Lou."

"Now Look. I . . ."

"It's OK." She cuts me off, suddenly smiling and seeming more human despite the hardness she has so carefully cultivated into the ambience of her character.

"No—wait a minute." I say. "I don't know you. I

was just trying to be polite. I was trying to live up to my
end of the bargain here. I don't need this. Excuse
me—Miss?"

I hold my finger up to get the attention of the wait-
ress.

"I'm sorry. Really."

She's smiling sweetly now. Trying to soften.

"Listen, why don't you come back to my studio.
Let me show you my work. I just get frustrated with the
public. OK? You seem like an decent guy."

"Well." I can see she's trying to diffuse the situation. "Why not?"

I've already blown the evening. Maybe she feels
the same. Might as well salvage something out of it and be
on my way. We take a taxi to her loft. During the ride I
attempt to reestablish the tone my Aunt Bea would have
approved of. "So what kind of art work do you make?
Like landscapes or portraits?"

She starts to give me one of her looks that I recognize by now to mean *you fucking moron*. But she stops
herself, smiles, touches my arm, probably an imitation of
some feminine gesture she has observed in a movie.
"You'll see."

Keys. Deadbolts. More keys and locks. Clicks,
chain rattling.

Inside it's dim, grim. There are smells—dankness,
urine, maybe cat, maybe human. I've seen these places
before. The entrance to the building doesn't always reflect
what you will find when you get to the loft. She pulls back

the noisy steel accordion that guards the inner cage of the freight elevator. I hear sounds from other tenants of the building: thumps, bumps, the creaking of water pipes, raised voices and the higher pitches of children, before everything is drowned out by the mechanical sounds of the elevator. Its ancient motor, labors to hoist us to the 4th floor.

Inside, we two art-lovers are quiet. The lift comes to a lurching halt, delivering us to a terrifying steel door with its own cadre of locks. Its dark in her studio, a big space illuminated only by the windows: neon signs, street lights—until she punches a button bringing up the interior lights with a loud industrial clunk.

I can see her entire life in this room, fridge, table, chair, TV, toilet. I am a little taken aback by the toilet. It's right there in plain sight. The space is forty by thirty feet, with twenty-foot ceilings. The bank of industrial-zone windows open outward allowing in the pleasant night and the unpleasant traffic and sirens. Probably a warehouse or factory in the days before the artists took over.

"Well?" she says.

"Um, I don't see anything that I recognize as art at this point."

"It's there. How can you miss it? Make yourself a drink and look around." She indicates a table that contains several kinds of liquor, tonic water, club soda and a half-liter of Pepsi. "I'll be back in a minute."

I watch her walk back to the gloomy corner that holds the toilet, drop her pants and sit to (I assume) pee. I avert my eyes although I'm aware that there is no real need for this courtesy. I hear her flush. I glance back to the toilet and she is gone.

Seeing no paintings or sculpture that I would rec‐ognize as art, I can only assume that the art which, to Roxanne is so obvious, is contained in the large domed structure in the center of the room. I approach the thing and cautiously enter its igloo-like tunnel. I hunch my way to the point at which it widens into the dome. The interior is light. The space seems vast, much bigger than the exte‐rior indicated. I can't go any further in, as the floor is not so much a floor as it is a lake. The surface is glassy, black. It could be as deep as Lake Superior. There are sounds in here. Like breathing. A slow and steady background heart‐beat makes the structure seem alive. Out in the middle of the lake a brass bed squats. The bed seems to be resting on rather than in the water. Stars are reflected in the lake's surface. I look up again. There are no stars in the "sky" only the pale white glow— and clothing: suit jackets, pants, shirts, socks, and underwear.

Lots of them.

I bend down to touch the water and send ripples out from my fingers. The stars shimmer as the ripples pass. I have to pee. Suddenly, I like the idea of peeing into the bitch's artwork. So I do. When I zip up and turn around, a beautiful woman stands before me with her arms folded over her thinly covered, perfect breasts. She smiles at me and I feel my face flush.

"Is this more the picture you had in mind?" the

woman asks in Roxanne's familiar voice. "I'm Stephanie."

The spiky black hair has been traded in for fluffy golden curls. She poses seductively in a teddy. She approaches to kiss me. I find that I can say nothing. She holds me at arms length and waits for a reaction. Something is not right here. But I already knew that. The question is, what will I do with this knowledge when every man's dream-come-true seems to be offering herself to me.

"This . . ." I wave toward the dome and its contents. "This . . ."

"Art," she offers, snuggling up to me now in a soft fleshy way.

"Art." I admit. "What is it? What's it for? What's it mean?"

"It's for you. I made it for you—and the others."

"What others?"

She waves her hand to the clothing rack that is the domed ceiling.

"See that empty space. That's reserved for your soul. All the others, those are the souls left here before you. Now I need yours."

"And just how are you going to get my soul?"

"You are going to fuck me and leave your clothing here. Then I will have your soul to hang up there with all the others. I have other clothing for you to wear home. Then this piece will be finished and I can get started on a new piece. So get those clothes off and get out there in that bed, Buster."

"Then I'll be out a soul," I say.

"Look," she says, still sweet, still the sexy new Stephanie, but I can feel the old Roxanne edge creeping back. "It's just art. I get what I call your soul, to put in it. You get—fucked. So stop being a big pussy and get out there."

I can't help myself despite the fact that this is all wrong. I'm aroused and—well . . . there it is. She leads me by the hand as we walk on water like twin Jesuses, out to the bed. I'm reluctant at first to make the unearthly trip, prepared to swim if necessary but under the inch of water there is a hard surface.

"Tar," she tells me. "The stars are little lights strung through the tar."

"Couldn't we be electrocuted?"

"Nah. It's on a nine volt DC transformer."

So it *is* all art. I'm not really in danger of losing my soul. There is an explanation for everything.

Afterward, as promised, she sends me home in other clothes.

What an evening. I don't even know what to think. All I know is: I feel funny—sort of empty.

Crime
and Punishment

Autumn

It was exactly the kind of day that had dislodged him from the city, the weather at least. In town, November's reflective gray streets morphed into grayer buildings, rising until their post-modern domes and arches interfaced with the atmosphere and disintegrated.

Here also, it was cold, wet and gray, but the land, as green as county Clare, and only 50 miles from the nearest big city, stretched away from him until it folded itself into the river valley. From his cantilevered deck, he could not see the river, but it revealed its location unmistakably, by the layer of fog that levitated, just above the rounded edges of its steep banks. An unknowing stranger might easily be fooled; might amble down the gentle hillside into this fogbank. The first surprise would come as a sudden replacement of the ground beneath his feet, with 150 feet of air, as he hurtled past the limestone palisades at 133 feet per second. His final surprise of course, after the rush of air from his own lungs and the one that passed his ears, would be the splash—that he himself, would not hear.

But Martin had no intention of walking down to the palisades this morning. His intention was to return once again to chapter 17. He was stuck on chapter 17. Some mornings, just to get the creative juices flowing, he read through chapters 15 and 16 as a sort of warm-up, tweaking as he went, changing a comma here, cutting a sentence there. But invariably, he hit a Berlin-style wall at chapter 17. He was stuck at the point where Maggie and her dog came running from their ancient Appalachian farmhouse. *She shields her eyes against the uncontaminated October light. The droning swarm of low-flying B-17s causes the ground beneath her feet to throb, sending the pulsations up through her chest, certain that one particular tail-gunner, on his way from Texas to Hitler, is returning her wave.* He sipped his coffee and fumed at the landscape. His 40 acres were perfect. But it wasn't his 40 acres that troubled him. It wasn't his 40 acres that undermined his path to the river of creativity, immersing him instead, in schemes of acquisitiveness and destruction.

"Thou shalt not covet thy neighbors wife," said Kara, creeping up from behind and slipping her arms around his middle. "Nor his manservant, nor his maidservant, nor anything that is thy neighbor's."

"I don't want his fucking, fat wife, or his butler or those little thugs of theirs. I just want every sign of their existence bulldozed off the face of this planet. Only that."

"Why don't you forget about them and try to get some work done?" she said. "I've made fresh coffee and I'm working on some cinnamon rolls. I'll bring them up after a while." She kissed the back of his neck and returned to the kitchen.

He was already aware of the cinnamon rolls or something of that sort, as the aroma from the interior had followed his wife out onto the deck. Feelings of guilt, a difficult-to-dislodge remnant of his Lutheran upbringing, flooded his atheist heart. Guilt in its many guises, could be triggered by several different catalysts. Family guilt accompanied every phone conversation with his daughter. The invitation by the local writer's workshop to judge the short fiction entries, ninety-five percent of which dealt with the dredging up of poignant family histories, triggered guilt about his mother's final years. And if the stories were not about memories of Mom, they were about Ol' "Red" or "Blue" or "Yeller"— tales that always brought the "old dog" guilt home to bear. Maybe Ol' *Rex* would have had a few more good years in him had he not trustingly climbed into the back seat for one last trip to the vet's. Would he, Martin, want to be put down, just to bring an end to the biting and tearing of all the hair from his arm or leg?

Today it was "love thy neighbor guilt." He took one last look out to the sodden November and returned to his house. Along the way he had a minor attack of *out-of-place-house* and *out-of-place-intellectual-urban-invader-of-Appalachia*—guilt. He and his architectural spaceship, hewn from clean, white, foreign-substance panels and an acre of glass, stood out against the hills, the farms, the oxidizing pick-ups and sawmill ruins—like a planter's wart on a princess.

But at his computer in the upstairs studio, the small window— the only small window in the house—provided him with a view that once again, stemmed his trickle of creative thought. The instructions to the architect had been clear: big windows for the majority of their acreage—hills, river gorge, few—and small windows—on the side toward the neighbor.

He schemed. He plotted. For now, he set aside his guilt.

Kara entered with the tray of rolls and the coffee carafe. She eased into the comfy chair next to his desk with her own roll and coffee cup, to read the morning paper—quietly—as he worked. But seeing him brood over the window, she knew there would be little work again today.

"You just keep picking at that sore, don't you?" she said. "Why don't you just close the blinds."

"You know," he said, "I *moved* here to look out the window. If I had wanted to keep writing in an enclosed room with no access to the world, I could have stayed in the city—in the basement. This screen looks the same whether it's in Bermuda, New York, or Mars. When I look up now and then, I don't want to see a wall—or *that*."

Kara rose to share the view with him. The sun had broken through the mists of morning and a blinding glare now shimmered off the few reflective surfaces: chrome, glass shards. The remainder of the field of view the small window afforded, was filled with the non-reflective rust and oxidized paint of a 1976 Chevy Nova, a 1982 Pontiac *something*, truck tires, axles, a transmission or two, fly-wheels, carburetors, and the infuriating primary colors of plastic big-wheels, plastic trucks, plastic tires, plastic steering wheels, and—Martin was certain—under all the plastic automotive make-believe, were surely *plastic* axels, transmissions, flywheels and carburetors. This pile held the artifacts of the current master of the neighboring property as well as the young hoarders-in-training who were even now, being groomed to continue their father's legacy of creativity-jamming. Beyond this accretion, out of view, unless one leaned over the computer monitor in order to take in the entirety of the affront, lay the house itself with its own internal collection of refuse, animate and inanimate.

As they watched, an article of paper trash caught a breeze, floated up to the level of the window and swirled in an eddy for a few seconds—just to insult him.

"I'm going to do something," he said.

"Like what?" said Kara. "That man could break you like a stick."

"Sometimes a man's gotta do what a man's gotta do," the scrawny writer replied, looking himself up and down in the full-length mirror attached to the closet door. The silvery glass revealed a middle-aged white man, a clean individual who had not made his living by hand and shoulder. A weak chin, from which, a turkey wattle, depending to the point of its connection with his neck, seemed to sum it all up. His adversary, Winslow Perkins was a somewhat of a specimen—6 foot 2 or so, forty-ish, and trim. When he folded his arms and glared menacingly at Martin, he resembled an Oscar—except for the baseball cap.

The few times they had spoken over the three years since Winslow had moved into the old Johnson place with his family and its refuse, Martin had noted the difference in their jaws. Martin had not owned a proper chin since the fifth grade. Winslow's jaw, the entire lower quadrant of his face from the point at which it was hinged, pushed upward and forward at him, a shovel, threatening to scoop him up and toss him into the drainage ditch at the roadside.

"I'm going over there to have a talk with him," Martin explained to his wife and his reflection. But he didn't go just yet. He piddled with some odd jobs until about noon when he heard the first warm-up shots. He had almost forgotten—it was Sunday. Pop . . .pop . . .pop-pop-pop-pop. Boom Boom Boom Boom.

Silence.

He could never picture in his mind, the weapon that made the thunderous booming. Did Perkins own a canon or a bazooka?

Ratatatatatatatatatatatatatatatatatatatatatatatatatatata tatatatatatatatatatatatatatatatatatatatatatatatatatatatatatatatata tatatatatatatat.

Little Jeannie Perkins always practiced on Sundays after church.

Two counties over was the *Big Shootout*. Folks came from out of state, some from as far as California, to pay a hundred bucks, awaiting their turn to blast away at a lineup of Cadillacs, Ford Tauruses, Chevys, and what-have-you. And little Jeanie, only sixteen, it had been reported proudly in the *Herald Leader*, was the women's overall national-champion machine-gunner.

Martin was not quite sure what feminine skills were needed in order to qualify as a women's machine-gunning champion, but he felt certain that her aptitude in that regard was accompanied by a certain lethal aspect.

*

He watched from his window as Jeannie Perkins, accompanied by her proud father, walked back to the house, her weapon now enfolded in its neat black case. This seemed an opportune time to make his approach, to face Jeanie, her father's terrifying jaw, and the rest of the Perkins heathens.

Winslow himself answered the door. Actually he didn't so much answer the door as make his silent appearance at the door.

"Good afternoon, Mr. Perkins . . .Winslow. May I call you Winslow?—Yes, well the reason I've stopped by, is to discuss with you, a proposition."

Hearing no objection or for that matter, no encouragement, he continued:

"It is this: I'd like to buy your property."

Perkins began to close his front door.

"Now just a minute, Mr.—er—Winslow. Hear me out, please."

Martin could see past Winslow Perkins into the dim, cluttered interior. A dog or two, lay about disinterestedly in the part of the house he could see. A TV droned somewhere and Mrs. P stood silhouetted against a window, the newest Perkins edition resting on ample hip. She looked on, timidly taking in the scene unfolding on the front porch.

"I want to make you a decent offer for your property. I'm prepared to pay $155,000 for the house and your five point six acres. I have the plat here. Picked it up from the courthouse."

Martin held the sheet toward Perkins, pointing at the lines drawn there.

You see that your driveway inters . . ."

The door began once again to close.

"One-seventy," Martin quickly updated his original offer. "One-seventy-five."

Slam.

*

"Well?" Kara asked.

"It didn't go all that well," Martin told her, "but at least they didn't shoot me."

"Or break your nose and crumple up your glasses." She paused. "So he didn't go for 155?"

"Or 175. That damned junk pile isn't worth 25, but," Martin added, "every man has his price."

"Or every woman," said Kara. "Listen, I had other uses for the money from Mom's estate, but I'll pitch in what I can."

"You don't have to do that."

"It's OK. It'd be worth it if it would get you back to work."

Kara convinced him that she should make the next attempt.

"You've already pushed your luck. And Winslow's unlikely to hit or shoot a woman."

*

Kara waited for the absence of Perkins' old Chevy flatbed from the driveway. A shirtless kid answered the door.

"Your mom home?"

"Mom!"

Mrs. Perkins emerged from the darkened house to

stand shyly just inside the door.

"Yes?" she said, in a voice so faint that Kara had to strain to hear above the din of the TV.

"Sally," said Kara, "I'd like to talk to you about my husband's offer."

"I don't know nothin' about that," the woman said.

"Look," said Kara, handing her a slip of paper, "I've written a figure. This is a good offer."

The figure she had written was on a different piece of paper than the one she and Martin had composed together. That piece was crumpled in her other pocket.

The woman read the number and looked up at her neighbor with popping eyes.

"Would you like a cup of tea?"

"That would be very nice," said Kara.

Kara tried to ignore the squalid interior and shut out the noise from the TV. The kids had turned the volume even higher, to drown out the voices at the table. The 16-year old women's national machine-gun champ hovered silently at her mother's elbow as the negotiations continued.

"It don't seem like the place is worth that," Mrs. Perkins said, shaking her head at the slip of paper.

"Listen," Kara said, "You could get something really nice for your whole family—a nice place in town—maybe build a new house somewhere around here even."

"Lemme see that," boomed the male voice from behind her.

Winslow Perkins, his approach masked by the screen of noise from the TV, appeared at his wife's side. He examined the number and turned his gaze on Kara. Without looking away, he said to his wife, "Pack your bags, Momma."

Kara came through the door smiling and clearly

expecting to be high-fived. Martin, somewhat suspiciously, reciprocated her gesture, with the gentlest of hand-slaps.

Kara indicated the need for a low-five as well, followed by a hip-bump. But Martin cut off the celebration at her approach for a leaping chest-bump.

"How'd you do it?" Martin inquired.

"Don't ask. But I'll just say this. I made him an offer he couldn't refuse."

Spring

Martin watched the workers from McIntosh's Sod Farm unfurl their lush rolls. It reminded him of a slow motion nature-shot of a frog's tongue, sent out to snag an insect lunch. The fresh carpet of grass glistened in the spring sun, obliterating every trace of Winslow Perkins' house and trash heap. Martin didn't even mind the now distant chatter of machine-gun fire, barely audible from Perkins' new place, a mile or so down the road. Each afternoon, Winslow Perkins honked as he sped dustily past in his shining, new blue Silverado.

At a safe distance away now, The Perkins were steadily assembling a fresh pile of trash outside their new —as Martin called it— "quadruple-wide." Perkins, apparently bent on some new get-even-richer scheme, had indeed expanded his collection to include a bright yellow backhoe and an equally bright yellow bulldozer. But Martin didn't care about any of this, as long as it didn't spread into his field of view.

Summer

Martin had deleted chapter 17 in its entirety. He rewrote it as what he now considered his "revenge" chapter. *The bombardier allows the tail gunner to peer down through his sight. But he has trouble identifying his house. His house, he knows, will be hard to find, tucked back into the holler. He looks for familiar landmarks. Then he remembers . . .the old Perkins place was destroyed by a tornado.*

Then he sees them. Two tiny figures run into the clearing, the woman circled by the running, leaping dog.

The work flowed easily now and by July it was finished. He and Kara shared a bottle of champagne on a blanket overlooking the palisades; his urban-invader guilt gradually subsided as he convinced himself that this was where he belonged.

In August they flew to Vancouver where they boarded the *Norwegian Princess* for a ten-day cruise of the Inside Passage. They toasted each other from their deluxe-balcony suite as calving glacial slabs slithered into the bay, sending ice-cluttered swells rolling toward their deck chairs. Martin examined the glowing tip of his Cuban *Don Tomas*, thankful that their northern neighbors did not honor the trade embargo.

*

Something wasn't right.

"Did you miss the turn?" Kara asked.

Martin looked back over his shoulder as he threw the forest-green SUV into reverse and backed up to re-examine the road-sign. Sure enough—county road 218. He drove slowly back up the road but the view had changed in the two weeks they had been away. In place of their house, the gleaming architectural wonder, overseeing the pristine hills and river, there was a flat, grassless vacancy—except for the still-visible concrete edges of a backfilled walkout basement. A gravel driveway still led from the road to the bare dirt where their house had stood. He pulled into it just as a blue pick-up sped past and honked once.

They got out and walked over the recent site of their home in silence.

Another message, about as subtle as a severed horse head, was written in the spent cartridges and shotgun shells scattered over the site.

At that moment Martin knew that he *was* out of place after all.

Yet, there was a certain symmetry to the entire matter, Martin thought. He imagined the bare dirt patch covered over with green. With his house and Perkins' house gone from the landscape, the scene would appear much as is must have looked to Daniel Boone when he had first laid eyes on it.

Before they drove into town to register for the night at the StarLite Inn, they stopped at the McIntosh Sod Farm to place another order.

Me and Donnie
and Travis

After work let out on Friday, me and Donnie stop in down at Tina's to throw back a few Buds. I'm kinda worried about Donnie ever since his wife, Charlene run off with that lawyer fella. Shit. I guess that must've been two or three years back. Seems like nothin's fun for him no more. Take last week. We went to the race up in Darlington, and you'd a thought it was a union meeting or somethin'. Then there was Connie, works third shift. Hell, everybody I know's had a piece a that. So me an' Dale fix him up with 'er but even Connie can't seem to cheer him up.

Seein' somebody like this sorta makes you appreciate your own situation. Like me, sometimes I complain about my ol' lady. She gets on my case every time have a few too many beers or stay out past three or four, but hell, she's not so bad now that I come to think of it. We sit there not talking much, and my imagination gets the best of me: I picture comin' home early some day and catchin' Sharon ridn' some guy on the couch in front of my new 42 inch plasma TV. (I don't actually got one a them yet, but I got my eye on one down at Sears. Just wait'n for the price to come down a bit.) Anyways, the only face I seem to be able to put on the guy is Donnie's lawyer.

"I got the first round," I tell Donnie, and order us a pitcher. I try to cheer him up with some blonde jokes but he only grins and stares off into space. It's like he's really somewhere else.

"Randy told me he got him a new truck," he says

at last. "Well, not exactly new. He got it from Wanda up in personnel, a Dodge Ram. You know, she don't have no use for it since her husband dropped dead over in Shively. Randy says he practically stole it from her."

"Good for him," I say.

There ain't much I want to hear about that son of a bitch, Randy. Wish he'd been the one dropped dead, Shively or any damn where.

We're quiet again for a while and my mind goes back to the lawyer and my ol' lady. Actually, I start to get kinda excited thinking how it would be, watchin' them two goin' at it like a couple a porn stars, but then I start getting' pissed off again. Maybe I'd shoot the two of 'em. But no. That never works out the way you picture it. Probably just wound him or get nervous and shoot myself in the foot. That's what happened to Pete Snyder. Then Pete ended up in jail for six weeks and the guy run off with his wife anyway. Pete's only got two toes now. Looks like a seven-ten split.

Hell, I don't even remember where I got that gun hid. 'Sides, Sharon don't let me keep it loaded, and I gotta stash the bullets in a different place so the kids can't find 'em and shoot each other accidentally or nothin. Fact is, she's been after me to get one of them trigger locks.

I says, "Shit, Sharon, trigger locks is for pussies — somethin' them soccer-moms thought up at one a their PTA meetings."

Say some nigger breaks in your house. First off, you gotta find your gun. Then you gotta find the bullets,

Then you think, 'Now where'd I put that damned trigger lock key?' Hell you'd either be dead or robbed blind by the time you got all that shit together. 'Course if you was to come out of it alive you'd . . .

"Hey," Donnie says, kinda snappin' me out of my little daydream. "I got this thing back at the house," he whispers, lookin' left and right. "It's still a secret right now but I think this could be my ship come in."

Now Donnie, he ain't a real talky type 'til he gets a few beers in him. Then he starts telling me this crazy shit about some big mystery he's got hid up at his place. Somethin' that could make him famous all over the world.

"Hell," he says, "I might be on Letterman. You never know. Then my ex'd take notice."

He sorta gets a dreamy look.

"She'd be sorry she ever run off like 'at," he says.

"I gotta get up early tomorrow, Don. Sharon's got a shitload of 'honey-do' projects for me around the house. First off, I gotta rent one of them tillers and root up her garden. Then she wants me to spray that bleach shit on the deck out back. . ."

He ain't listenin' though. He just goes on with this bullshit about his big secret, but my mind keeps goin' back to that lawyer and Sharon. I bet that's why she wanted me to keep that gun unloaded in the first place. Soon as I get home I'm gonna find that sucker a load it.

"I'm not shit'n ya. It's down in my basement. Come on over an' see for yourself, but. . . ." he says real low, checkin' all around, "you can't tell nobody about this.

I'm revealin' it when I'm good an' ready."

"Don't worry," I says. "My word's good as my name."

He gives me a kinda funny look on that one, but we pick up a twelve pack and drive out to his place.

On the way I start feelin' pretty sorry for myself about Sharon runnin' off with that lawyer. Bet she'd take the kids with her. Just leave me with the cat. Hell, pretty soon I'd be as pathetic as ol' Donnie. That's all he's got in the world is that cat of his.

I can't cook. Who'll do the laundry? I know I'm supposed to separate the whites and the dark stuff but I ain't doin that. It'd probly be OK though. Just throw 'em all in there together. I'll eat sandwiches — maybe order pizza every now and then. Hell, I'm still young. I can probly find somebody new. Gotta lose a little weight and get a more modern type haircut. Shit. That's gonna be a lot of trouble. And I hate goin' out on them dates. You gotta be Mr. Polite all the time and spend half your damned paycheck just to get laid once a month.

By the time we get there, we each throw'd back a couple more brewskys. Donnie takes me straight to his basement door. We stand at the top of the stairs and look down into the dark.

"Be kinda quiet," Donnie says. "He spooks sorta easy."

At first I don't see nothing 'til my eyes adjust to the dim light. Then I hear a little sound, a sort of rattlely, purry sound and I see . . . it.

"Jesus Christ!" I start to bolt, but Donnie grabs me by the arm.

"It's OK. He likes people. He's real nice. Sorta friendly really."

"Is that what I think it is?" I ask.

"You seen the movie right?" Donnie says.

"Yeah," I says, "I seen the movie, an that fucker there's the scariest son of a bitch in it. How'd you get one a them anyway? I thought them suckers had to be cloned or extracted from some pearl or somethin.'"

"Amber."

"What?"

It was amber, not a pearl. But I don't know where he come from. Just showed up one morning and I could tell he was real hungry. He kinda sniffed at me and looked at me real friendly-like. Seemed real, you know — like smart, so I give him some raw hamburger. An' you know what? He ate that right outa my hand, then he went in the bathroom an drank real big outta the toilet. After that he just curled up over there in the corner and went to sleep."

"How you know he's a *he* anyway? How can you tell with a thing like 'at?"

Donnie smiles and gives a whistle and the damned thing comes right over to him and sorta lays its chin across his lap. — Me, I'm backin' away. Its head is twice the size of Donnie's, and that row of sharp little teeth seem to spread out in a kinda grin. It's sizin' me up the whole time Donnie's makin' over it— scratchin' it and such — watchin' me with them cold little eyes, like it's thinking I know something that Donnie's too dumb to figure out.

"Looky here," Donnie says and lifts up its back leg.

Sure enough there's its big ol' schlong.

"Yep," I says, "guess he's a boy alright. Donnie, now dammit, you can't keep a thing like that in town. Why hell, if the neighbors get wind of it they'll have the cops over here faster'n you can piss on a candle."

"I know, but . . . I trusted you. Now you can't say nothin . . . besides, he's got real good night vision, so I can take him out back after dark and play stick with him. Nobody'll see us at night. Hell, Charlie, he's just like a big ol dog."

"Yeah" I says, "'cept for the scales and that dang claw thing. He could gut you with that son of a bitch just on accident. Shit, Donnie, you remember how Brutus used to get so excited sometimes he'd knock me over? Cracked my rib that one time I come down on that rock.

"Yeah," he says, "sorry about ol' Brutus."

He looks away real quick when he catches me wipin' at my eye.

I'm kinda quiet for a minute — sorta envious of Donnie I guess, have'n a thing like this.

"Well," I tell him, "all I'm sayin' is just be careful. This is one of them cases where a little too much excitement could kill a man."

Just then Donnie's cat Fluffy peeks around the corner. Fluffy arches his back and growls. But the creature perks up at the sight of the little fur ball.

"I gotta get home now, Don. It's gettn' late and the ol' lady's probly already pissed off as it is."

"All right" he says, "but remember, you can't tell nobody about this. Not yet."

We close the basement door and me and Donnie and the cat say our goodbyes.

*

It's damned near impossible not to mention this incident, but I don't want to cause nobody no trouble so I keep it to myself. Donnie keeps me updated at work whenever we can get away from the others.

"Travis is great," he tells me. "He's so damned smart."

"Who's Travis?" I ask.

"You know," he whispers and bugs his eyes out at me.

"Ohh. . . .Why Travis?"

"I named him after my little brother . . . he died when I was five . . . luekemia."

"I'm sorry," I say.

"Well you know . . . that was a long time ago but he kinda reminds me of him."

I maintain silence on this matter. We sit for a moment without speaking.

"Say," Donnie says, "you wanna go to the Brickyard 400 this year? I got a extra ticket."

"Where's the seats?" I ask. "Last time we had to sit

inside the third turn."

You got a view of about twenty feet of track, banked above your head. I spent most of the time staring at bare asphalt then about ten seconds of roar and blur followed by long stretches of blank pavement.

"Northwest Vista," he tells me.

"Shit. That's good."

From the Northwest Vista you can see the north shute, turn four, the straightaway and the pit entrance.

"I'm in," I say. "What the hell was we talking about?"

"Travis," he says.

"Oh yeah. So, how's he doin'?"

"Aw he's great."

"You remember that yippy little dog, lives next door, belongs to that bitch of a neighbor?"

"That one that barks all the time?"

"No, I'm talkin' about the dog."

Donnie's pretty funny sometimes.

"Used to bark," he says with a wink. "Travis and me was playin stick out after dark and that little shit was out there in her yard, bein' quiet for once. I think it seen Trav and decided not to make a big deal out of it. I didn't even know it was there until I threw the stick over that way and I seen Travis veer off and grab something. Next thing I know he come runnin' back and drops the little fucker's head at my feet. You could tell he was real proud at what he done cause he looked up at me like he'd just fetched the paper."

"Damn!" I say.

"You know what he did then?"

"What?" I says.

"He went back and got the stick."

We both laugh at the thought of this.

"Hand me another beer," I say.

"Know what else?" Donnie says, crackin' the tab for me.

"What?"

"The little dog's name was Amber."

"Well shit, Donnie," I says, "that Travis is a smart fucker. Even got a sense of humor."

"That's right," says Donnie. "even appreciates . . . *irony*."

Donnie just about laughs his ass off over this comment but I don't get it. I give him a sort of pity laugh.

*

It's a couple weeks later when I drop in at Donnie's place unannounced with a twelve pack. He's glad to see me once he's peeked out through the curtain to make sure I don't got nobody with me.

"Gotta be careful," he tells me. "The ol' bat next door's been suspicious ever since that damned Amber disappeared. Stood out there calling for about twelve days. Hell, it was almost as bad as the damned barking. Lately, I seen her snoopin' around in my yard, looking for clues, like. I thought about letting Travis shut her up too."

We both chuckle at the thought. I can just see Travis stand'n at the back door scratchin' to get back in the house with that claw of his, kinda grinnin', holdin the ol' lady's head in his mouth.

Just then the cat, Fluffy, comes scrambling through the room, skidding around corners with the raptor hot on its heels. Me, I'm thinking I'm about to witness somethin' ugly, when Fluffy jumps up onto the back of Donnie's new green-leather LazyBoy and turns to face off against the monster. Travis pulls up short, staring at the cat, thumpin' that tail on the floor. The cat sorta stands on its hind legs and reaches out with both paws and slaps at Travis's head. Then it jumps right over him. The raptor bites at it. Sometime he catches the cat and tosses it in the air. You can tell it's all playful though. The two of 'em run over furniture, turn over lamps, break some cups and shit.

"Oh I know," Donnie says, "they just about wrecked the place but they have such a great time, I figure what the heck?"

I look around then and notice big tears in the couch cushions . . . stuffing bustin' out of 'em. Just about every piece of furniture looks like mine did the day after that fuckin' Randy broke in my house. He found out I'd been poking that girlfriend of his. What the hell was her name? Began with a C. Candy or Cindy. Karen! Nice piece a ass.

"It's that damned big toe of his," Donnie says, "Rips the shit outta stuff." He smiles, shaking his head at the creature like a proud daddy. "But ain't that about the cutest thing you ever seen?"

Just then Fluffy calls an end to the game of chase and starts scratching on the door-frame. Donnie kicks at the cat.

"Damned cat," he says, "gonna take the house apart board by board."

I notice on the floor under the door-frame, a pile of sawdust that Fluffy's scratching has produced. I'm thinking to myself, first off, if it was my place I'd at least clean it up, and second, I'd get rid of that damned cat. Course, it's obvious Donnie don't mind playin' zookeeper. Guess he's just got a soft spot where it comes to his pets.

We settle in to watch the first half of the Lakers game. The raptor comes over to me and lays its big head in my lap. It looks up at me with them hard little eyes. I'm not real comfortable with this, having all them teeth so close to my you-know-what. But Donnie puts me at ease.

"He wants some of your beer."

"Oh," I say and start to give him some.

"Travis! You Leave him be now. You go get your own beer."

The animal slinks away and I hear from the kitchen the click-click of its claw on the refrigerator handle. It returns with the beer in one a them little front claws and brings it to Donnie, who opens it and pours the contents into a disgustingly filthy bowl on the floor. The raptor laps it up and lays down right there at Donnie's feet for the remainder of the game. Got its head on Donnie's shoe. Damn! I sure would like to get me one. At least it wouldn't be fuckin' no lawyer.

Hell, what am I thinkin'? Be just my luck, mine'd be dumb as a jar of loose change.

"So," I says to Donnie, "can't he open it hisself?"

"Well I showed him how I do it with my teeth, but I guess he's sorta scared he might break one of his."

*

Funny how you get used to somebody no bein' around much any more. People get busy with their own stuff. Then one day about a week ago Pete points out that he ain't seen Donnie for a while. So after work I decide to go over there. The door's locked and I don't see nobody. I go around back and find several windows busted out and the back door hangin' by one hinge. I go inside.

"Donnie? Don?"

Man, what a smell. There's no sign of Donnie and the place is really a wreck, tables overturned, everything smashed up. Naturally, it occurs to me that there may have been foul play. Like maybe somebody broke in. But just then I see a movement. It's dark in there, but I make out Travis — just sittn' there in Donnie's LazyBoy.

"Hey Buddy," I say "Where's ol' Donnie and ol' Fluffy?"

Travis cocks his head at me. He looks sorta hungry.

Only thing I can figure is this: Donnie and the cat must have split. Donnie hadn't been all that happy since his wife left him. And he didn't care much for his job. Oh well. One thing for sure, I can't leave poor Travis here on his own like this.

"Come on boy," I say and coax him out to my truck. "The ol' lady'l just have to get used to you. An' you know what?"

Travis cocks his head again.

"We got a cat I think you'll like."

O'hare

She had always expected a music sound track—to
her life. It ought to be that way. You get up in the morning
and your theme is playing softly in the background as you
brush your teeth. Something like *Peter's Theme* from
Peter and the Wolf, but more up to date. Not a full orches-
tra, but light strings with a digital drum overlay—maybe.

She turned the stalk on her fake Levelor blinds to
look out onto the dreary new day. This is where she should
see the fabulous sky-line—should hear those fantastic
opening clarinet bars. *Rhapsody in Blue.* What else could
possibly work here?

There really *was* a fabulous sky-line though—magical in some light conditions. From the North Pond Café
for example, on a crisp fall morning pause in her eight
mile run through the park and along the lake—it could be
OZ. Unfortunately, her not insubstantial income, was
insubstantial enough for this pricey OZ. The magical vista
remained just on the other side of the brick alley-wall of
the apartment building across from her window.

Still, on the way to work she often conjured up the
kind of *An American in Paris*-business-class strain that
invokes the hustle and bustle of her great city.

"OK," she thought, "so it ain't Paris, but it is a
damned great city."

In the evening, of course, there would be romantic
music, something to have a candlelight dinner over, or dinner at a restaurant with that special person.

"What would Dad pick for this scene?" she asked
her reflection as she carefully applied bright red lipstick,

pulling in close to examine her work, making a cursory check for new wrinkles. But she couldn't really come up with anything to fit the romantic evenings, maybe because they hadn't worked out all that well. But she gave it a stab anyway. For now she would go with Smetena. Peter, her ex-husband, had always said that she should use *Pictures At An Exhibition*, but she knew that was all wrong. He had just been trying to impress her with the only memory he had retained from the few days he had actually attended his Music Appreciation class. Sometimes she wished her dad had never given the son-of-a-bitch a passing grade.

This morning, the music was something dark, heavy—maybe *Night on Bald Mountain*. She stood at the corner of Sheridan and Oakland, braced like the three others there, against their bitter OZ's penetrating, icy winds. Where was the cab? Did they not say they would be there at 6:15? She stepped out into the street yet again to search into the teeth of the wind tunnel that is Sheridan Road. From the letterbox picture of her big eyes, the only exposed slot of flesh between stacks of stylish wool—hat, scarf, ankle-length coat and boots—flowed tears. The tears were for the wind, but they were also for herself, for the injustice of the cold, and the struggle of life here, so far from her mild, southern, red-neck-college-town-upbringing from which she had so needed to escape.

She punched the speed-dial on her cell phone.

"Hello," Merril said.

"Hi, it's me, Dad."

"Where are you? Sounds noisy. You on your way to the airport?"

"No . . .well sort of," she said. She didn't want to cry at her dad, so she sucked it up and just cursed for him. "The fucking cab was supposed to be here twenty minutes ago. I'm afraid I'm not going to make my flight. Is Mom there?"

"She's in the shower. You know, I'm doing the

dog-walking cat-feeding stuff and trying to get ready. Our flight out isn't until 1:30 but we've got that two-hour drive to the airport. Where are you?"

"I'm at the corner at Sheridan. It's so cold." She stamped her feet.

"Who is it?" Christine asked, poking her wet head out of the partially opened bathroom door.

"It's Traci."

Christine seized the phone from her husband, flashing him a stern look as though he had been hoarding the instrument, keeping it all to himself, trying to snatch her baby.

"What's wrong? — Well, maybe they're just running late. . . .OK, OK . . .now calm down."

Merril and the dog observed the exchange. Christine, with her hand over the mouthpiece, whispered "She's crying."

Traci braced against the wind and spoke tearfully into her cell phone.

"I don't know what to do. There won't be a bus. I'm freezing my ass off here. This goddam place. — I'll call you later. Don't worry about me. I'll catch a later flight."

Christine shrugged and handed the phone back to her husband.

"What?" Merril asked.

"She's crying and cold. Her cab didn't come, and she calls me—three hundred miles away. What can I do?"

"She needs her mommy."

Fifteen minutes later Traci called back—from a cab this time.

"This lady, standing at the corner, let me share her cab." She smiled at the woman who was still in the cab with her so that she felt she had to whisper.

"There were other people there waiting. I don't know why she offered to share her cab with me."

"Could it be," Christine suggested, "That you were the only one sobbing?"

Traci needed this brief respite. She needed to meet her mom and dad for R&R. Needed to be a dependent child again, if only for the five days of make-believe that was a Southern California vacation in January.

She bought the Trib at the newsstand. The five-dollar airport sticky bun and the five-dollar airport coffee were somewhat comforting as she tried not to review her life, tried not to do the biological math that added up to one failed marriage, several failed relationships and the fuse, smoldering toward a fizzle in her empty womb. Thirty-five now. What did it mean to be thirty-five. Just a few years ago, she would have called a woman in her mid thirties a *lady*. The nice lady who had obviously been touched by her Sheridan Road tears, was, now that she thought about it, maybe only a few years older. Maybe forty-two. Soon *she* would be forty-two.

"Where do you see yourself in five years? Ten years?"

How many times had she been asked that question by unconcerned human-resource types in her, what was it now, ten years of job-hopping. Five years ago, she was a beautiful young wife, a modern professional woman with a charming, go-getter husband, a home, two cars and a garden. So from any reasonable point of view, the last five had been a downhill spiral. What now? No man. No home. No car. Only a few flower pots in the windowsill overlooking the alley.

What would things have been like if she had followed her urges. Well, actually she had followed those. Byron was, she had to admit, the love of her life. Handsome, funny, sexy, passionate, hard-drinking, brawling, self-pitying, infuriating, ne're-do-well Byron.

Instead of continuing down that road, she had *set-*

tled for a successful young business-type. Traded in the
passion for the comfort, the security. But. . .she had
thought there would be *some* passion. Two . . .three times
a week kind of passion. Maybe she had expected too
much. Maybe lusty Byron had been way more than your
average Joe. She didn't know what to expect from the
average Joes. Certainly there had been no one else since,
who seemed to stir that kind of passion in her. Or who
seemed to harbor it *for* her.

Sex, sex, sex.

Involuntarily, she turned to the man who sat next to
her at gate C-14, reading his own copy of the Trib. She
needed to check his reaction, in case she had absent-mind-
edly blurted those three "sexes" out loud. He didn't seem
to notice anything unusual. She smiled at him when he
turned to look at her.

He was pointing now at an article in the paper,
punching his finger into it.

"You know," he said. "You know who runs them. I
mean this company. You know don't you?" The man, who
had at first appeared normal, not too bad looking even,
now frightened her with his bugged out eyes.

"I'm sorry," she said. "What company?" She
looked at the headline he poked at. Something about Wal-
Mart. "Oh."

"Eye ran," the man said.

"Eye ran? . . . Oh, Iran."

"No, I had no idea," she said.

"Oh yeah," the man said. "Lots of their stuff comes
directly from Iran, or through middlemen who are fronts
for them. Do you have a cat?"

"A cat? Well, I did, but he died."

"That's too bad. But cat food, litter," he was getting excited, punching at the paper again, "It all comes
from them. Didn't know that did ya? Every time you
empty the litter box, your helping them acquire weapons-

grade plutonium."

"Really."

"That's right. Say . . .where you from?" He was smiling now. Now that he had elucidated his political saavy for her, he was ready to make his move. "You're from the South aren't you? Let me hear you say something. I just love that accent."

She recognized the music which, at that moment accompanying her life. It was the theme from the *Twilight Zone*.

"Oh," she said, suddenly looking at her watch, jumping up. Clearly, she had forgotten to do something, misplaced something, had some last second important something that needed her urgent attention. "Excuse me," she said, sprinting away from Gate C-14 and the lunatic she had looked to, if ever so briefly, as a hope.

They were always so fascinated with the accent. She was after-all—exotic. A beautiful exotic bird. A cockatiel settled into the midst of all these sparrows and grackles. Once she opened her mouth, her plumage became visible. But that charm always wore off, sometimes after only a few dates. Or it might drag painfully on for a year or more until the words had to come out. The words that always came from her bright red lips in their musical southern flavor.

"Where do you see this relationship heading?"

How many times had she asked that question over the past four years? She didn't wish to make that calculation right now. She was trying to lose herself in the crush of people at gate 15, just out of sight of gate 14, and the crazy man who inhabited it—but still within earshot of the flight announcements there.

The answer to her question, at least the immediate answer—was always the same. Silence. In that non-response she always found the information she sought. Often, after a period of composure, five . . . ten seconds as a rule, some stumbling retort was forthcoming. But she knew that her warning shot had been fired, and that was usually all it took to send the guy packing. These were not brave men.

There would be a friendly dinner or two, followed by lengthening periods of absence. Absence of phone calls, uncomfortable lulls in conversation at dinner, finally a drop-by to pick up a few things that may have been left at her apartment. She usually had this stuff neatly packed in a box or bag, ready for a 100 meter relay-style baton-pass.

One particularly cowardly gentleman seemed to have decided to abdicate his shoes, a jacket, and some toiletries. He must have paid at least a one-hundred-seventy dollar penalty for a new cell phone plan.

Wait. She was getting all (as she called it) *twerked* up here. She needed one of the anxiety pills Joyce had prescribed for her after their last session. One of the pills that she remembered now, were in her carry-on. The carry-on that she had left sitting next to the wacko at gate 14.

She eased her way over to the gate and spotted her bag. Well that was a relief. With the new security situation, it could have been confiscated or worse. The threat insinuated by her abandoned portmanteau might have shut down the airport. She began to worry about security. If it was that easy to leave a bomb in the airport, was this really a safe environment?

"Get a grip."

She calmed herself with her emergency tune, another selection from *Peter and the Wolf*—the Duck.

She sneaked behind the bank of fake-leather seats. Some poor slob was sitting in her former seat, being chatted up by the loon who was now prodding the other man's newspaper. Probably babbling away at him about *eye ran* or *eye rack*. Neither individual seemed to notice the bag. She was mildly surprised that there was not a whole string of luggage, hurriedly jettisoned by passengers who had fled the guy's rantings. She slipped successfully behind them and retrieved it.

Still ten minutes before they would probably begin boarding. She checked out the Starbucks kiosk. By the time she reached the end of the line, she wouldn't have time to drink it. Each lucky customer, having at last reached the *order here*, intentionally took an inordinate amount of time with his no-fat, chocolate, double latte—tall, no wait—short, no . . .sorry . . .tall—thinking carefully—and slowly—about each additional ingredient. Then he would look back with apology written all over his face before turning away from the line-up to smile mischievously to himself.

Men.

The men she liked, really liked—the ones she hung out with—were handsome. And—they were kind, caring, sensitive to her feelings, built like brick shit-houses—with sculpted muscles, chiseled jaw lines, firm little butts—and queer as three dollar bills. They were everywhere . . .at work, at the gym and especially in her neighborhood.

"Honey," her dad had said to her just last week, "I don't want you walking around there by yourself after dark."

"Dad," she had explained while walking home, talking on her cell, "I could walk down the street naked, and no one in my neighborhood would even notice."

She needed her mother. Needed to shop for even more shoes—with her—in sunny La Jolla. A new pair of shoes might take the sting out of her most recent failure at amour.

Craig.

Craig who wasn't even cool—closer in fact, to *born nerd* than cool. Craig had shown more interest in his car stereo than he had in her. After investing months into Craig—the trip to Wisconsin to see his sick mother, an entire Saturday test-driving SUVs, and another Saturday shopping for special woofers, Craig had balked just like all the others at the *big question*.

More disturbingly though, Craig was prepared with a ready answer. None of this *let's be friends-two final dinners-one last drink* stuff for Craig.

"You just don't bowl me over," he said. "I need to be swept off my feet, knocked for a loop."

Truth was, now that she came to think of it, she would have loved nothing better than to do all three to the son-of-a-bitch. Maybe from behind the wheel of his woofing SUV.

When the boarding call came, she waited until there was no one else left before boarding. She stuffed her carry-on into the overhead rack and took her seat. Seat 22 A.

A window seat—next to the lunatic.

"Well," the man said. "Looks like we meet again."

She scanned around the overbooked flight for a nonexistent escape route and relaxed.

"You sure had to take off in a hurry. Then I noticed your bag was gone. I was afraid somebody might have stolen it. Did you get it back."

"Yeah," she said, smiling her wide-mouthed, red-lipped, big friendly smile. I got it OK." She was tired. The thought of seeing Mom made things seem easier. She could let her guard down. She never ordered drinks when flying.

"It can dehydrate you," all her gay friends advised.

But this time she ordered two. They would help pass the time with this guy who just loved hearing her talk. When she was tired, when she had a drink or two, the south just poured out of her, all the words leaning casually on each other. She hummed to herself while the man talked, Foster—*My Old Kentucky Home*.

A Christmas Story

Since Mother passed away I've taken up driving again. Cars are so handy. You can get groceries and beer. In the afternoons I like to sit and watch when the school lets out. In my car, I'm just like the others, waiting.

The policeman said, "You can't let him get behind the wheel."

Mother always reminded me of what he said whenever I asked if I could drive. But she's gone now. It was an accident, really. At least *I* think so.

I had to come home early today. Usually I stay and watch until the last ones leave. The little girl I'm interested in has some kind of after-school activity. I don't know what it is but she comes out when it's almost dark wearing a tight-fitting stretchy thing.

Its almost Christmas and I like to have something nice at Christmastime.

You know those sounds that get in your head—the vibraty ones?

Today it was the one like a machine gun. That's why I decided to come home early instead of following her.

Ratatatatatatatatatatatatatatatatatatatatatatatata tatatatatatatatatatatat.

On and on like that until I thought I might go crazy. Sometimes it goes on for twenty minutes and then that backbeat starts—you know that boom, clank, boom, clank, boom, clank.

Before long the message comes through. At first I think it's just the noise, then I hear it.

Takerhomenow-Takerhomenow-Takerhomenow.

The adoption people wouldn't let me have one of the Chinese girls. It surprised me, really. I knew they wouldn't let me have one of the regular ones but I figured the Chinese ones are harder to get rid of and they'd let me have one. But they said no and called the police. They told Mother too, and she was very upset with me. She cried when the police talked to her about that. I don't see what's the big deal though.

Now that she's gone I'm going to get one. Not a Chinese one. I'm going to get a regular one. The one in the tight stretchy thing at the school.

She's going to be my angel.

The lady on channel 3 looks like Mother. Since

Mother died, I watch channel 3 a lot. Tonight she's reading letters from brothers and sisters who write in to give their testimony—the lady I mean, not Mother. Brother Daniel comes on with an electric guitar. I think the lady and him are in the same room or at least the same building but she never gets out of her chair and he never moves away from his microphone. It looks like they see each other though, and she says she's real glad he's here tonight because he has a good testimony.

I'm thinking about giving my testimony when I get my girl.

Brother Daniel sings but I can't quite follow it with all the vibraty noises going on, so I take a beer outside to the hole. I don't like to work on it until after dark. It's nobody's business really.

I can't sleep very well because of all the good ideas I get.

They always wake me up at about 4AM—the ideas I mean. I try to stay in bed because that's supposed to be good for you but I can hardly ever stay there past 5:30. I have to write my thoughts down in my *journal*. That lady at the hospital told us about journals. I got right into it—like I had been born to do it. She was very interested in mine. At least that's what she told me. She says she'd like to borrow my journals for something she's writing up but I wasn't born yesterday. I'm going to write a book one of these days and I'll need all of my materials.

I had to move my bed into another part of the house. It was easier to move the bed than all of my journals, but once I get them transcribed into the computer I plan to burn them. That way nobody can get my ideas and plagiarize. Then I'll probably move my bed back in.

This looks like the day.

Angela—that's what I'm calling her—Angela—she's waiting for her ride. The rain has made it darker.

"Hello there, young lady."

She doesn't answer me.

"I'm Billy. They sent me from church. Said I was to pick you up. Your mother can't make it."

Damn she's a cutie. She holds her books real close to her little body. Those eyes of hers. Wow. Just look at those lashes.

"I'm not supposed to talk to strangers," she says.

"Well, I know that. Your Mommy told us that at church. She said you'd probably say that, and for you not to worry because it was the church people this time and you shouldn't be afraid of them. Do you know about Jesus?"

She shakes her head.

"You do? Well, we give Jesus our testimony at the church. Do you know the lady on channel 3?—Oh, well then—you know whose birthday it's going to be real soon, don't you? No? Well, it's Jesus. Christmas is his birthday and he's got presents for you at the church so you come on now. It's OK."

"You're fat," she says.

"Well," I say, "that's not a very nice thing to say. Jesus wouldn't like to hear you say that. The people at church told me to give you this."

I hold up the pair of pretty angel wings I got at the Wal-Mart. She comes closer to look but then backs away.

Now here comes a car.

"Well, you know what? I can't wait here all day. I gotta get goin' now. Gotta decorate for the birthday. You don't have to say anything about this to anyone. I'll see if they'll hold your presents for you though. You can get them tomorrow. Bye now."

She waves at me but I don't stick around to see if she gets in the car that's coming.

The next day I don't drive to the school. Angela might have mentioned my car, you know, like what it looks like and all, so I just walk over there and sort of stand behind a tree. But she never comes out.

We've got a room in the basement that Mother said was the family room before Daddy left. I never knew Daddy and Mother didn't want me going down there. But since she passed away, I do. I cleaned it up and I'm making it special for Angela. I made a Christmas scene down there. They call it a crèche. It has a stable and some religious-looking people and a manger and some fake goats. Angela will be my angel.

The hole is deep enough now. I'll be glad to get Mother out of here. It's starting to smell pretty bad.

I don't see Angela again. In fact, some policemen grab me there at the school and they don't let me even go back home. I try to explain about the crèche but they won't listen.

*

I sort of remember being here from before. They let me listen to music the last time.

"Now try not to move," the lady says. "The first series will take three or four minutes."

"This looks different than before," I say, "bigger."

"That's right," the lady says. "This is the open MRI. It's for *bigger* patients. Now lie still and we are going to take some pictures."

"Of the inside of my head, right?"

"That's right, now lie still."

"Don't say *ground squirrel* to me. Did you say that? I thought I heard you say that."

"No, we didn't say ground squirrel. Now here we go."

I'm pretty sure I heard ground squirrel. It might not have been the lady though. Here come those noises.

Ratatatatatatatatatatatatatatatatatatatatatatatatata

tatatatatatatatatatat.

Boom, clank, boom, clank, boom, clank. This machine matches those other sounds—you know the ones I mean.

Now here comes the message. Can't quite make it out. Wait it's:

Littlenegroboylittlenegroboylittlenegroboylittlene-groboylittlenegroboy.

I guess I have put on weight. Angela said I'm fat. This lady thinks so too.

But now I know what to do. Everything is so clear now. It wasn't the angel. When I get out of the machine I'm going to get a baby Jesus. A little Negro Jesus. He will look good next to all that red.

And—I'm going to try to cut down on my calories and get more excecise.

Dan Darrin and Darlene

"Are you coming to bed soon?" Beth asked.

"Pretty soon," said Darin. "I want to work on these plans for a bit. We've got a meeting with the Chesapeake Group in the morning and we think they're about to give us the go-ahead."

"I'm getting pretty tired of your working every minute. We never spend any time together. Whatever happened to quality time?"

"You're the one who wanted a new house, remember. Now that we've got it, someone's got to pay for it, and until I see evidence to the contrary, that someone is me."

He poured a cup of coffee from the carafe and disappeared into the dark hallway leading to his office, mumbling under his breath, sloshing coffee as he walked.

Beth gave a shrug and started for the bedroom with her tea and *Bon Appetite* when she was startled by a knock at the door. She peered through the peephole to see a familiar face. With some trepidation, she opened the door.

"Mr. Marsh . . . uh, Dan . . . how are you? Come in. I'll tell Darin you're here."

"Where's that li'l rascal?" said the elder Marshall, scanning the apartment behind his daughter-in-law's back.

"You know, it's pretty late. We just got Austin in

bed for the night."

"I jus wanna see'im fer a minute, Beth."

"Dad. How ya doin?" said Darin, materializing into the foyer from the darkened interior. "Would you like some coffee?"

Dan Marshall waved the offer away with a look that indicated disgust for the beverage.

Beth slid between the two generations of Marshalls, giving her husband the bug-eye as she mounted the stairs to take up a defensive position at the threshold of the latest generation.

"I wanna see li'l Astin."

"Austin."

"Right. Ausin."

"Dad, he's in bed. Does Mom know you're here?"

"She . . .that . . ."

Dan Marshall's eyes wandered over the walls of his son's new home, noting how his daughter-in-law had laid claim to the spaces suitable for artwork. He thought of registering a complaint but stopped short of asking what had become of the three paintings — his paintings — that he had given them as wedding presents, birthday presents, and most significantly, his grandson's Christening present. Beth had shown little in the way of gratitude.

"Thank you so much Dan, but I'm not sure where we would hang such a large painting."

"Like every other Philistine," Dan thought.

The high-ceilinged interior his son had designed, with its museum-like white walls that could easily accommodate Picasso's *Guernica* with room to spare, soared above Dan's head. What a perfect venue this clean archetype of modernity would be for his art. But in place of its simple contemporary composition, interlaced with embedded poetry and references to political and religious protestations, were bourgeois accoutrements of the middle class: smallish framed reproductions of Marc Chagall, Monet, and the ubiquitous *Sunday Afternoon in the Park.*

Dan put an arm around Darin, waving an unsteady finger at the fake Seurat.

"Ya know," he said, "Thass not foolin anybody."

Darin turned to look at his dad, then drew back when the older man's potent exhalations wafted past his nose.

"They got the real one down at the Art Institute ya know."

When Darin turned his head he saw that his father's hand was bleeding.

"Dad, what's wrong with your hand?"

Dan removed the arm from his son's shoulder and scrutinized the appendage, seemingly without recognition, as if it had only generated itself there since his arrival.

"There's not a drink in it," he said. "Waddya got?"

"I'll get you a Band-Aid," Darin said.

"Nope. None of them fancy drinks for me thanks. A gin and tonic'll do jus fine. In fac, les jus make it straight gin."

Dan headed for the liquor cabinet as Darin loped up the steps to get his father a Band-Aid. But at the top of the stairs Beth intercepted him.

"What's he doing here? I thought you were going to tell him not to come back."

"I had a talk with him. It's not that easy you know. He wants to see Austin. I think we should . . . "

"Oh no. He's not coming up here!"

"Shh. He'll hear you."

From downstairs they heard the sounds of clinking ice cubes and the closing of the freezer door.

"I'm calling your mother to come and get him," Beth whispered.

"No, no, no. Don't do that," he whispered back with some urgency, "I'll get him calmed down and call him a cab."

When Darin returned with the Band-Aid, he found his father on the couch, channel-surfing.

"Here ya go," Darin said.

Dan turned with a bewildered look.

"What? Oh yeah." Dan said.

The old man took the Band-Aid and opened it with some difficulty, applying it to the wound on his meaty right hand.

He frowned at the hand and took a sip of his gin.

"Little disagreement with one of the sculptors. Bastards."

Thursday, Darin knew, was his dad's regular night with the art crowd down at the *WaterWorks*. Dan and the sculptors almost always became physically adamant about their viewpoints, arguing for hours about the relative merits of three-dimensional versus two-dimensional work. Most of the painters and poets maintained a humble demeanor around the big, noisy, hard-drinking, hairy, leather-clad, knife-carrying, jackbooted sculptors. The women among them were especially frightening. But his dad had never been one to back down from these brutes . . . lone defender of the gentler arts.

Dan was, after all, thought Darin, every bit as loud, hairy, and obnoxious as the 3D crowd.

He remembered as a boy, being dragged to one gallery opening after another. The evenings usually started out pleasant enough, with lots of congratulations, hand shaking and general schmoozing of the blue-hairs with the cash. But wine flowed freely at these events — sometimes harder stuff — and the nights usually ended in some kind of altercation, especially if his dad's arch-enemy

O'Connor was present, as he almost always was. Whether it was Dan's show of oversized abstracts or O'Connor's exhibit of *his* slick and colorful fiberglass sculptures, they always included each other on the invitation list. It was as if the work could not stand on its own merits. One of them had to show the other, in public, what a success he was. Down at the *WaterWorks*, the painters sided, albeit quietly, with his dad, and the sculptors aligned themselves with O'Connor. This was certainly not the first time his dad had shown up with some kind of aesthetically inspired injury.

"Was O'Connor there?" Darin said.

"Bastard!"

"Dad, you know I've got a meeting with clients at 9:00 and Beth has to be at school by 7:45. We really need to get to bed soon . . . so finish your drink and let me call you a cab."

Darin could never let him know about the beautiful pink and green fiberglass spiral they kept hidden in a basement storage room. The wedding gift from Frank O'Connor had become a point of contention between Darin and Beth. She had the perfect spot for the piece and wouldn't mind at all, the idea of showing her admiration for it in front of her father-in-law. Darin loved the piece too, but it would have to stay put until the old man was out of the picture for good.

Dan stood up, wobbling a bit.

"I don't need no stinkin' cab goddamit!" he yelled.

"Where the hell's my paintings? Look at this shit for God's sake. You're a fuckin architec' an' ya got these fuckin' reproductions of the 19'th fuckin' century all over the fu . . ."

Beth stormed down the steps.

"I'm not having this in my house! I want you out of here now!"

Darin stepped between the two combatants, trying to calm his father while holding back his wife's advance like a

coach trying to break up a melee among rowdy players.
"Aw, Beth," Dan protested, suddenly pathetic, with a gesture that sent gin and ice flying across the couch.
"Get out!" she screamed, "now."
Austin came running out of his room clutching a blanket and rubbing his eyes.
"Go back to bed, Hon," Beth said.
"Grampa!"
The little boy ran down the steps into his grandfather's arms.
"How you doin you li'l scamp?"
"I got a new big-wheel, Grampa."
Suddenly the child pulled away from his grandfather's stubbly face.
"Grampa, you smell bad."
Darin lifted the boy away from his father's grasp and Beth snatched the child up, hustling back up the steps just as the front door opened and Darlene, Darin's mother, stepped in.
"Dan, let's go home now," she said in her most soothing voice.
"I ain't goin nowhere!"
"Come on now. Can't you see what you're doing here. You're drunk."
"I ain't drunk!
'Come on now, Hon. Let's go home."
"No!"
'Why do you have to do this? Do you have to make some kind of scene everywhere you go? . . . What happened to your hand?"
"Aw, it's nothin'. That bastard, O'Connor."
"You know what, Dan?" Beth interjected, "Frank gave us .
. ."
"Beth!" Darin snapped, giving her the slit-throat sign, except down near his waist. It was an abbreviated version of the well-known gesture, shielded from his parents' view by his body.

"You're ruining our lives," Beth yelled. "I'm sick of it."
The raised voices floating out into the night beyond the
open front door had attracted the attention of a neighbor.
"You're ruining my night too," the man shouted across the
darkened lawn.

Darlene stuck her head out the door.

"Why don't you go back in the house and mind your own
business?" she screamed before Darin could manage to
close her words in behind his own front door.

"I come to see my granson an I inten to see more of 'im."
With that he lunged toward the stairs and began a slow,
heavy charge toward his daughter-in-law, who stood
fortress-like, at the top of the steps. By now, Austin had
reemerged from his bedroom and was peeking fearfully
from behind his mother's skirt.

At the moment Dan's charge met the stone wall of Beth's
resistance there was a heavy grunt, followed by a topsy-
turvy conjoined roll of the two adversaries as they tumbled
down the steps. Upon reaching the landing, surprisingly
unhurt, Dan looked up from his prone position, past the
blue pant leg, past the black leather belt and holstered gun,
into the scowl of a police officer.

The cop mumbled something into his shoulder and
a second officer appeared.

"Everything OK here sir?" the first cop asked the
younger Marshall.

Dan stood up painfully and brushed himself off.

"We're fine, officer," Dan explained, "just a li'l
understanding."

"Right," said Beth, "he can't even talk. He's a
drunken jerk, and I want him off my property,"

"Beth!" Darin tried to restrain his wife, who was
attempting to charge with flailing fists toward Dan.

"Ma'am, please lower your voice and calm down," said the second officer.

Austin was bellowing now as Darlene tried to silence him, cooing and crushing the child to her heavy-duty bosom.

"Everything will be fine, Officers," Darin said. "It's just a little problem. I think we've got it worked out." The two cops scanned the lavish contemporary interior. They exchanged a look.

"All right, but if there is anything else, please don't hesitate to call this number." The first cop handed Darin a business card.

"You sure you're all right, Ma'am?" he asked Beth, who was now sobbing quietly in her husband's arms. She nodded in the affirmative, not lifting her gaze from the polished hardwood.

The two cops turned and walked back to their car. Darin watched them get in as the neighbors squeezed the light from their cracked doors back into their houses. He shut the door and for moments there was only awkward silence, punctuated by gasping inhalations from Beth and Austin.

"You look good, Darin," said Darlene making effort to return normalcy to the scene. "You've put on a little weight. I hate to see you so skinny."

"What's that supposed to mean?" asked Beth. "I know you think I'm a lousy cook. I just happen to want our family to be healthy. We eat healthy food instead of greasy, artery-clogging meat. We respect animals and try not to kill them just to satisfy our bloodlust."

"Beth!"

"It's OK, Hon," Darlene said to her only child, "She's always been a little bitch, right from the start. She thinks she's better than us."

Beth snatched Austin away from his grandmother and scampered up the steps with him.

"He's been eating meat somewhere, Bitch," Darlene yelled. "Maybe at his girlfriend's house."

Darlene smiled, patted Darin's tummy and gave him a wink.

"Mom, Dad, this has been a very difficult evening. Could you please just go on home and I'll call you in the morning after my meeting."

"OK, but you know . . . you could do better than *that*." She rolled her eyes toward the top of the steps. "You were always the best looking boy in your class, and you're an *architect*."

Darlene whispered the word as loudly as one can whisper and closed her eyes with reverence for the title her son had earned. Darin's father stood swaying in the doorway.

"Thass right," Dan concurred, "fucking architec."

The older couple leaned into each other now, Darin's mother offering support to his wobbly dad. At last Darin managed to coax them out and send them toward their own home.

"Good night, Dear."

"Night, Mom."

He stood for a while luxuriating in the silence, and in his own numbness. Finally he managed to move toward the kitchen where he poured himself a large scotch. Just as he was pouring his second one he heard two light beeps of a car horn, followed by footsteps on the stairs. Beth appeared in the foyer with the sleeping Austin in one arm and a suitcase in the other. She didn't look at him. He didn't try to stop her.

He watched his wife step out the door with his sleeping son, and heard the cab drive away.

He finished the second drink before walking into the bedroom to look in the mirror. His mother was right. He had gotten fat. He pulled his shirt up to reveal the disgusting paunch. He turned to his side. He could hardly believe how *thick* he had become. It had crept up on him. It wasn't just the burgers he sneaked at lunch. He had stopped exercising. When was the last time he had gone for a run? Three months? He got down on the floor and did sixty sit-ups. He had to stop and rest at fifty. The final ten were very difficult.

He sat at the table a while longer. It was 12:15 by the time he decided to put on his running gear and go for a five-mile run down by the lake. He had to stop and walk a few times. When he returned, he half expected to find Beth and Austin back in the house — to find that the entire episode was a dream.

He poured himself another drink. Now that Beth wasn't here, he felt free to pursue his other vice. He fished back behind the cleaning supplies under the sink for the pack of cigarettes he had stashed. He lit up. Damn, that felt good. He smiled, remembering the words of his friend Casey: "There are only two things in this world that taste good: fat and cigarettes."

He thought over his options. Maybe his mother was right. Maybe he did deserve something better. He *had* been the best looking boy in his class, and now he was after all, an *architect*.

His parents — he didn't know what to think about that relationship.

"The hell with all of 'em," he said aloud to himself.
He went down to the storage room and returned with the O'Connor piece. He cleared a space for the sculpture in the entrance foyer and stood back to admire it.

Dog-man

Guy walks into a bar with a parrot on his shoulder.

"OK," bartender says, "I'll bite. What'll it be?"

"Scotch, Barkeep," parrot says. "Straight up. Somethin'nice. A single malt. Got any Macallan, eighteen year?"

The bartender hesitates.

"What? You deaf, Mac?" bird says.

"Uh no. We, uh . . .the closest I got is a Glenlivet, twelve year. That OK?"

"Yeah, that'll work," parrot says.

"*You* have'n anything?" the bartender asks the bird.

"That *is* for me," parrot says. "You got a real small glass, you know like a thimble or something? I have a hard time with them big tumblers."

"Sorry." The bartender shrugs.

"That's all right," bird says, "just put it down there."

The parrot indicates the bar in front of him with his wing tip.

"I can sip at it."

"Well, what about your friend? He want anything?"

"What time is it?" parrot asks.

"3:30."

"Better just get him a cup of coffee if you got any made."

The bartender looks back at the pot. Frowns.

"Been sittin' there all day," he says. "It's pretty rough. Won't take but five minutes to make a new pot."

"That's OK," parrot says. "The rougher the better. He drives the getaway car. Gotta keep his head on straight if you know what I mean." The bird snickers.

"Getaway car?" Bartender asks, bringing the coffee.

"That's right," bird says. "Oh, I forgot to tell you. This is a stick-up."

"I thought this whole thing was a joke," bartender says. But then he sees that the bird ain't kiddin'. Something about those cold little eyes. The way he cocks his head to the side to keep you under surveillance while he sips at his Glenlivet. Bartender makes a move for the button under the bar.

"I wouldn't try that, Friend," parrot says. "My buddy here's got a pretty good-sized hand-canon on him. Show 'im, Fred."

The bird-man pulls a long barreled revolver from inside his coat. Sets it down on the bar with a heavy thud.

"Now put the money in the bag nice and easy and we'll be on our way," bird says. "Oh, and by the way, I think I heard you say the drinks are on the house."

"So what'd the guy look like?" The inspector asks.

Bartender describes the man.

"Medium height, white, medium build, scar on his right temple."

"And you say he got away with about . . . ?"

"I don't know. I guess four hundred. Maybe four fifty."

"The gun?"

"Long barrel, like you'd see in a Western. Maybe a .45."

"Anything else you can tell us?"

Bartender can tell the inspector knows he's holding back.

The inspector's assistant's there now too. He's finished snooping around the place, dusting for prints, stuffing matchbooks in his coat pocket. The guy picks up a feather from the floor.

"Well, there is one thing."

"What's that, Sir?"

"He had this parrot on his shoulder," bartender says.

The inspector and his assistant exchange a glance.

The bartender notices a glimmer of skepticism but they say nothing.

"The . . .the bird. It . . ."

"Yes?"

"It did all the talking."

"We'll be in touch."

Guy comes into the bar with a dog—little dog, like
a Jack Russell mix. Bartender eyes 'em suspiciously.
     "Sorry, Bud. You can't bring that dog in here."
     Bartender's ready this time—finger already on the
button. But the guy nods. Says he don't mind tyin' the little dog up outside. Guy has a drink, gets his dog and
leaves. No funny business.

*

     "You're a total fuck-up, You know that?" parrot
says to his drunken friend. "We only got $400 from that
last job we pulled. And you sit there drinkin' it up. I'm
hungry!— Hello!"
     The man cringes when the bird yells into his ear.
     "All right. All right," the guy says. "I'll go down to
the corner store and see if I can find you something."
     Guy comes back three hours later. No bird food.
No money. Passes out on the couch.
     Bird's pissed off. Leaves.

*

     Bird walks into the bar alone. Same bar. Same bar-
tender. Bartender's wiping glasses and putting them away.
Bird's down real low, walkin' along below the level of the
bar. Bartender can't see 'im in the big mirror behind all

the bottles. Thinks he hears the door open though. Turns to look. Nothin'. But then the parrot jumps up onto the stool. Bartender spins, starts to move for the button—stops, thinking the gun-toting accomplice is somewhere just out of sight.

"Hey," parrot says, "calm down. It's only me. I'm clean."

Parrot holds his wings up to show the guy he ain't packin'.

"I left the no-good son-of a bitch. I'm sorry about the other day, Pal. But I'll make it up to you."

Bartender's interested.

"I got a proposal," bird says. "Got any more of that Glenlivet?"

Bartender pours the bird's drink.

"Wha'dya got in mind?" Bartender asks.

"I think we could make a little cash, you an' me." parrot says. "You know, go on TV— talkin' parrot and all."

"What's unusual about a talkin' parrot?" bartender says.

"Hey, guess you're right. I never looked at it that way."

Just then, the former parrot owner comes staggerin' through the door wavin' the .45. Points the gun at the bird just as the man with the Jack Russell walks in. Little dog sees the gun and goes for the guy. Guy's so drunk, the little dog takes 'im down, no problem.

Police arrive. "You're under arrest for armed robbery." cop says. They take the guy away in cuffs.

"Drinks all around," bartender says.

The dog-man, parrot and bartender toast each other.

"Hey!" the little dog says. "What about me?"

"I'll be damned," dog-man says. "I didn't know that little son-of-a-gun could talk."

"Listen," parrot says to the Jack Russell. "I got a little proposition for ya. Lemme buy you a drink."

"I'm all ears," dog says.

Mr. Kogovsek

"Wha'dya doing this weekend?"

"Aw, I don't know, nothing special. Maybe go up to the lake . . . if Brad feels like it. He says he's got a lot on his mind," said Debra.

Debra noticed the rolling of Sheila's eyes despite the screen of smoke released from her nearly clenched lips.

"What about you?" Debra asked.

"Oh, I don't have any plans. Might just kick back and watch some TV. Anything to get away from this place for a while."

Sheila studied her friend through the haze of smoke. Debra could tell Sheila was about to start in on her again.

"Look, Deb. What is it you see in that guy? He's never going to amount to anything. You work your ass off here and he sits home doing God-knows-what. Wake up. He's using you."

"I know, I know. I guess he's just my weakness. Every time I think I'm going to end it, I look into those blue eyes, and he starts sweet talkin' me the way he does . . . I just can't throw him out. You remember how it is. You were stuck with Paul for three years."

Sheila started to protest but Debra's raised palm cut her short.

"Oh, I know. He had a job and all, but we all knew he was runnin' around on you—I think you knew it too. Why'd it take you all that time to dump *him*?"

"Yeah, I guess you're right," Sheila said, "It's nice to have somethin' warm to come home to."

"Warm and stiff," Debra said with a little laugh.

"Sheila, Debbie! We got customers. I told ya's a hundred times . . .you can't both take your break at the same time. Now get to work."

"It's Debra," said Debra.

"OK then . . .Debra . . . would you please get table seven?"

"Table seven!"

"Yes, table seven."

Debra flipped her hair at Mr. Valentino, picked up the little leatherette wallet that held her order pad, and started in the direction of table seven. But without missing a stride, she turned a neat ninety-degree arc and pushed back through the swinging doors into the kitchen.

"Sheila, please don't make me go out there. You do it. *He's* out there."

Sheila went to the swinging doors and peered through the little window. At table seven sat Mr.Kogovsek.

"Oh no," said Sheila," I'm not takin' that on."

"Oh please," Debra begged, pulling on her friend's arm while flexing at the knee with a child-like display of protest. "I'll take a shift for you next week, anything, just . . ."

"What the hell's goin' on here?"

"Oh please Mr. Valentino, don't make us wait on him. You do it. Please."

Valentino peeked out into the restaurant. It was still early and only three tables were occupied, two with older couples, the only ones who ate before seven. But at table seven, sat Mr.Kogovsek. The suit he wore was the same one he had been showing up in, at least once a week for the last ten years. His nearly three-hundred pounds had stretched the seams in the back of his jacket until they were near the bursting point. His yellow-gray hair was still very thick, but greasy looking and . . . he smelled. But perhaps worst—was his attitude. It was never a good attitude, and what's more, he seemed to take pride in the fact that it was his.

He dined out, always alone, every night of the week. You just didn't know which night your restaurant would be hit. Tonight was the lucky night for Valentino's.

"Sheila, you take it," Valentino commanded. With that, he walked back into the kitchen where he could order and prod the cooks.

Debra watched from the swinging doors as her friend made the approach to table seven. She could make out the greeting from Sheila and some grumbled response from Kogovsek. As Debra passed by on her way to table nine she heard Sheila going through tonight's special.

"A grilled Alaskan salmon with a creamy horseradish sauce, peppers charred in the embers with a wasabi vinagrette and goat cheese in grape leaves with tomato and olive salad. Or, Sheila added, "you may substitute the kidney bean salad with walnuts and cilantro."

He forced each waiter to go through this routine although everyone knew that he would in the end, order the same meal he always ordered. Now she heard Sheila recommending a wine that might go well with each of the specials.

Debra took the drink orders from table nine, passing by Sheila as she was taking down Mr.Kogovsek's order.

"I think I'll have the pasta al fredo, and a bottle of the house cabernet."

"And your salad, sir? "

Sheila had already written his answer—the house salad, with the house vinaigrette served *after* dinner—before he gave it.

In the kitchen, Sheila and Debra looked out to where Kogovsek sat.

"How do you think he stays so fat?" said Debra. "That's such a huge meal."

"Must snack a lot," Sheila said with a shrug.

The man ate slowly, reading one of the several papers he always brought with him—the Times first, then the Post, then the Evening Gazzette. The restaurant was beginning to fill up now. They didn't want to place any of their other customers too close to table seven because of Mr.Kogovsek's body odor, but space was limited. You could tell customers noticed something was odd as they saw their names written on a list, and wondered why that particular table sat in an area that could have accommodated two more.

A young couple with two small children was seated at the table nearest Mr. K. When the little boy gave out a small scream, immediately hushed by the young mother, Mr. K shot them a glance and practically leapt out of his seat. When he had recovered, he reached under the table to retrieve the small cardboard suitcase he always carried. He opened it cautiously, looking all around to make sure no one could see into his precious case, coming up with a pair of what looked like headphones—bright red hearing protectors spattered with many little flecks of multicolored paint. He put them on and returned to his paper. The other customers were looking at him now, although trying not to be obvious about it.

Sheila disappeared through the swinging doors, returning promptly with a tiny box containing several sets of discreet little foam earplugs.

"Perhaps you'd be more comfortable with these, Sir," she mouthed at him.

He snatched two of them from her and bent to replace the big headset into his suitcase.

"Would you care to hear about our desserts tonight, Sir?"

"Yeah, what'd ya got?"

Sheila recited the list, saving the one he always ordered for last. He appeared to think seriously about the choices, asking her to repeat two of them before ordering.

"I think I'll have the chocolate sundae, one scoop of vanilla, no nuts, and make sure it's the chocolate sauce not hot fudge."

Valentino and Sheila watched from the kitchen, waiting for the next bit in the routine. They were not disappointed as they saw Kogovsek get up and walk around his table three times before bending toward his chair and initiating some kind of gesture-aided discourse with it.

At last, after eight or nine cups of coffee and his chocolate sundae, he paid up and lumbered out, leaving a dollar on the table for Sheila's efforts.

"Mr. V," Debra asked her manager, "why do we have to keep serving that guy? Can't you do something?"

"Well, he's been coming here since my brother owned the place. He's just eccentric. Besides, you know what everybody says."

"Yeah . . . I know," Debra said, "He's got millions tucked away under his mattress or buried in his back yard."

"Or," said Mr. Valentino, "we don't know what else is in that suitcase other than those headphone things. I've tried to peek in there when he gets them out. Once I even looked through binoculars from back here."

"What could you see?"

"Not much. He sort of shields it with his body. You can tell he don't want nobody seein' what he's got in there but I could sort of make out some white curvy shapes."

"Maybe he sells ivory on the black market. I bet those are tusks," said Sheila, joining in the conversation with a dreamy, faraway look.

"Yeah, said Mr. Valentino, "that's probably it."

*

"I'm home," Debra called out as she stepped in the door of her apartment.

There was no answer. She hung her coat and hat in the hall closet and walked through the combination living/dining area to the bedroom where she found Brad sitting on the bed, illuminated by the TV in his semi-conscious state—smoking a joint.

"With a smokey exhalation, he breathed "Hey, Babe," noticing her at last. "Want a hit?"

She took a pull on the joint and handed it back to him at the same time that she fell backwards onto the bed.

She knew she could, or should . . . do better than Brad. But he *was* a hunk— good abs, square jaw, ponytail—and he was harmless if you didn't consider having to be totally responsible for him, harmful.

"What did you do today?" she asked.

"Well," he paused trying to remember just how he *had* passed the daylight hours, "I did some thinking."

She was hesitant to broach the next subject. Would that be nagging? She really didn't want to be 'that person.'

"So . . . what about that job interview?" she said at last. "I thought you were going see about that band."

"Band?"

"You know, the band that advertised for a drummer. They seemed interested."

"Aw, Babe. They're so square. I was *big* there for a while. The *Kickers* were kick-ass around here. You know that. We were cool. I can't go back to playin' gigs at wedding receptions and the Elk's Club annual dance. I'm just waitin' for the right opportunity to come along. I need to be big again."

She took another hit off his joint and smiled as she slipped her hand over his washboard abs and into his pants. "I think you're getting big."

*

Afterwards, as they lay half propped against the

headboard, smoking a last *j* and talking quietly to the
accompaniment of a flickering, muted Jay Leno, she told
him about Mr. Kogovsek.

"Everybody says he's loaded."

"Really?"

"It's probably just one of those rumors that goes
around about any bum that folks see on a regular basis."

"But you said your manager knows him."

"Yeah, well, only because his brother used to let
him come in. After Frank died and Mr. V took over, I
guess he thinks it'd be bad luck not to carry on the tradi-
tion.

"Doesn't sound to me like the guy was all that
lucky for his brother. I think we ought to look into this,"
Brad said.

"Look into what?"

"You know, the money. Find out where the guy
lives. Let's go check it out."

"Brad!"

"Aw, Babe, I'm just curious."

*

"Mr. V," Debra said the next day, casually finger-
ing a pencil on the countertop, "Where's this guy live?"

"What guy?"

"You know . . . Mr. Kogovsek."

"How the hell do I know? Why do you ask?"

"Oh, I don't know, just wonderin'. I thought maybe
someone ought to look in on him. He seems like kind of a
sad case."

"Well aren't *you* the Good Samaritan."

Despite the lack of help from Mr. Valentino, Debra
was able to find Mr. Kogovsek in the usual way: he was
listed in the phone book. There was only one Kogovsek.

Chester A, 235 Abriendo AV.

*

They parked a few doors down from Kogovsek's house.

"I really don't know about this," Debra said.

"It'll be OK," said Brad, "I just want to check it out. Aren't you curious about those rumors?"

It was a modest neighborhood. The houses were neat and the lawns well maintained—except for one. Kogovsek's house was the champion of modesty. Unlike the rest of the quiet tree-lined street, his yard was treeless, but certainly not grassless. The grass and weeds were at least a foot high. There were no ornamental plantings of any kind. But you could tell that at some point there had been mowing, because clumps of yellowed, clipped grass, probably from the last cutting some weeks before, lay flattened on the sidewalk. Conspicuously, Kogovsek's house was the only one without a vehicle, either in front or in the drive. Debra knew he always took public transportation.

"If something should happen to Mr. K, I don't think he'd be missed," Brad said.

"What makes you say that?" said Debra.

"See how the only fences in the entire neighborhood are on either side of Kogvosek's lawn. Privacy fences. They don't want to look at it."

"I don't mean that. I mean what's going to happen to him?"

"I'm just sayin'. . . if something did, it wouldn't matter a hell of a lot to these people, I bet."

They sat there until it was almost dark. Except for the distant barking of a dog and the hum of many air-conditioners, the neighborhood was quiet.

"I'm goin' in," said Brad. He checked his watch. "The time is 9:15, August 12th, 2003."

Debra glanced around to see to whom this comment was addressed before giving him a funny look.

"What?"

"Nothing. I'm going with you."

She could tell he was about to object but seemed to
think better of it.

"OK," he said, "but let me do the talkin'."

They crept up to the porch, peeking in the window
nearest the door. They could make out Kogovsek's silhou-
ette in the dark room. The only lights came from the flickering television and the magma glow of the man's cigarette.

Brad knocked.

Debra heard the big man groan as he shoved his
bulk free of his chair. His resounding footsteps traced a
path to the door, which he opened cautiously.

"Yeah?" Kogovsek said, looking Brad up and
down.

Debra could tell Brad was about to launch into
some bogus reason for their visit when he was cut short by
Kogovsek, who had now also noticed her. She saw a spark
of recognition in his eyes.

"So," he said. He directed his comments toward
Debra, but shifted his eyes toward Brad. "Is this the drummer? Come on in."

Brad looked at Debra, who could only shrug in
response. They walked into the house.

"Watch your step," said Kogovsek. "Sorry, I'm out
of lightbulbs."

Brad took in what he could of the TV-illuminated
squalor and whispered to Debra, "It's probably just as
well."

Despite the warning, they both tripped over junk
on their way to the living room.

"So," Kogovsek began, "you must be art lovers.
It's good of you to come really. It's good to see that there
are still among the young, those who can appreciate something beyond the drivel that passes for the so-called *arts*
these days."

He nodded toward the TV.

"Oh, I know. You're asking yourselves, 'if he is so disdainful of television, why is it that he wastes his time with the medium? Why not do something useful with the hours he may have left on this earthly plane?' Well, I have to ask myself this very question from time to time. The answer is always the same. I am like the rest of them—lazy. Too lazy to find it within myself to create or entertain. It's much too easy to just sit passively in front of the idiot's bulb. That's why I've become so fat. It disgusts me."

"Listen Mr. Kogovsek," Brad began.

Kogovsek cut him short with a raised palm, "It's just *K* to those who would count me among their friends."

He reached down to his belly and grabbed a huge portion of loose flesh with both pudgy hands and shook. He didn't shake the handfuls of skin but instead shook his generous head causing his jowls to flop about audibly, reminding Debra, of a cartoon character.

"I wasn't always this way. Back in Cincinnati, in the old days, I was appreciated. Oh yes. They used to come. 'K,' they'd say, 'would you be so kind as to sign my program?' Or, 'It's not for me, of course, but for my little boy. He's a huge fan, but naturally he's not allowed to stay up until such a late hour.' But as you both are aware, that was before the moon landing."

By this time Brad and Debra had managed to find seats. Brad was actually lounging in a sling chair that he had emptied of its cargo of vacant snack food containers. Debra sat hunched on a wooden crate.

"Cincinnati became, shall we say . . . *embarrassed* . . . at my continued presence. Who was I, to embarrass such a great city? I thought at the time, 'well perhaps I should end it all.' But no. That would have been too easy . . . on them! After all, why should I let them off the hook? I know how it goes. One day, it's all such a crises. All the people are asking: 'Whatever happened in that Kogovsek matter? Perhaps we were wrong. Maybe we were too quick to judge.' And a week later it's all forgotten. Some new urgency presents itself, some war or celebrity murder, and soon they've forgotten all about poor Mr. Kogovsek."

Sensing a pause in the soliloquy, Debra raised a finger, and opened her mouth but she wasn't quick enough.

"And of course, there is my health. After my four years with British Intelligence—Oh, you didn't know about that did you? Yes. Four years of my life I gave to those unappreciative bastards. The Agent Orange took its toll. But I say, 'one must be thankful above all, for whatever health one retains. Still, the chemo is hard on me."

Debra thought she saw Brad begin to nod off. She knew he was trying to pay attention, but recognized his behavior from the times she had managed to drag him to the symphony, or the ballet, in an effort to instill a bit of culture, or more realistically to be seen by friends at a cultural event, in the company of her man. He would seem to be totally engrossed, as she noted by glancing peripherally, when suddenly he would jerk and emit a snort.

She nudged him now.

"So I said to myself, 'K, perhaps it's high time you . . .'"

"Shut up!" Brad said, suddenly awake. "Look at this place." He indicated his disgust with a sweep of his right hand, which now held a revolver, produced from the recesses of his jacket.

Debra was clearly surprised at this new twist.

"Brad! What are you doing?"

"I know you got money Kogovsek. Everybody knows it. And you're gonna tell me where it is . . .now."

With that, he cocked the trigger and aimed the gun at Kogovsek.

"No Brad!" said Debra.

Kogovsek smirked.

"What is that? A twenty-two? It's not that you couldn't get the job done with a twenty-two, it's just the way you immediately start waving the thing around. There's no introduction—no build-up. I don't feel threatened. Did you ever see the movie *True Romance*? No? Well there is a character played by Christopher Walken who speaks softly, but authoritatively to Dennis Hopper, sitting across from him. It's that whole softness, that politeness of the questioning, that builds the tension and implies the violence that you are certain is to come. Of course, Christopher Walken doesn't brandish a weapon because the two henchmen with him—see he—Walken, is the brains behind all this—they have guns trained on Hopper. Maybe it would be more effective if *you* did the threatening, and *she,*" Kogovsek indicated Debra, "held the gun."

"Yes," Brad said, rather excitedly, "I do remember that movie. It's great, that scene especially. How bout this?" Brad said, "*You* be Dennis Hopper and *I'll* count to three. Oh, and by the way, if you use the word *brandish* or *disdainful* again, I'll shoot you just for the hell of it . . . One . . two . . ."

"OK. OK! . . .That was good. You know, I felt a bit of a threat there. I just about peed my britches. That was really pretty good acting. Yeah," he shook his jowls again, "you had me sweating there for a second. You're going to be all right, Kid. . . . Debra, would you be so kind as to go into the performance room and bring my clubs? It's just through that door. But watch your step. I've taken the floor out."

Debra walked to the door Kogovsek indicated and opened it.

"The switch is to your left," he said. "That bulb still works."

Kogovsek turned his attention back to his tormentor. "Have you seen *Reservoir Dogs*?"

"Have I seen it? Just about twenty times. It's only my all-time favorite," Brad said. "I can't believe you asked me that."

Debra was surprised that Brad seemed to be getting worked up.

"You know the scene where Mr. White and Mr. Orange just about kill each other in that standoff early in the warehouse part?"

"Oh man! I love that scene. Orange says, 'you just about made me shit my pants I was so scared.'"

"Yeah," Kogovsek said. "That was the way I felt just now. Everything's a movie."

"You got that right, Bro," Brad said.

"I'm overjoyed that you two are hitting it off so well," Debra said. "Maybe you should move in together."

She flipped the switch, illuminating a space that was more like a shaft than a room. At first she looked up. The walls were white and extended to the regular room height of the ceiling. When she looked down, where the walls continued into the basement in place of the floor that Kogovsek, or someone had removed—she screamed—and backed away.

"Let's get out of here," she said to Brad.

"What is it?" Brad said.

"Let's just go. Now!"

Brad kept his eye and gun trained on the fat man, and backed his way to the opening. He looked down and saw on the floor, a snare drum on a stand, and a small cardboard suitcase. The walls surrounding these items were splashed and smeared with dried blood—lots of dried blood.

"Jesus," Brad said.

"Looks real doesn't it?" Kogovsek said. "Two parts Alizarin Crimson, one part Burnt Umber and one part Hooker's Green. It makes perfect dried blood. Of course you have to wait at least a day to get the proper effect.

Acrylic dries lighter."

"But . . ." Brad started.

"The bloody head print? A string mop works perfectly. The hands are obvious. I just dragged my hands along the floor."

"Wow!" Brad said.

Debra could see that he was truly impressed.

"Go on, Babe. Get the man's clubs."

"What clubs?" Debra asked, directing the question to both of them now.

"They're in the bag," said Kogovsek.

Debra descended the ladder that dropped into the shaft-like room and stepped toward the suitcase.

Up above, Brad made a finger-to-the-lips, *be quiet* gesture to Kogovsek, tiptoed to the door and switched off the light. Debra screamed. He flipped it back on and he and Kogovsek shared a good laugh over his little joke.

"You know," Kogovsek said, "when you backed away to look down there, holding the gun on me, you reminded me of something from a long time ago."

"Yeah, what's that?"

"Patty Hearst."

"Oh yeah. I know what you mean. The bank robbery film. That was so cool, the way the camera jerks cause it's a time lapse."

"Here," Kogovsek said, "try this."

When Debra returned with the suitcase, she did not appear happy. She watched Brad, who now cradled a toy machine gun, as well as the .22 and was doing some kind of strange backward, jerking moonwalk. Both men were laughing and congratulating one another over the ridiculous dance. She put the bag down and opened it. There were the mysterious white objects that Mr. Valentino had observed through binoculars.

She pulled one out.

"You mean these bowling pins?"

"Oh no," Kogovsek said. "Bowling pins would be much too heavy. Have you ever handled a bowling pin, my dear?"

"Watch it K, that *my dear* is dangerously close to *brandish* or *disdainful*."

"Sorry," Kogovsek said. Both men were smiling now. The tension seemed to have passed.

"Those are clubs. If you would be so kind as to bring them to me I'll give you a demonstration."

He took three of the lighter-than-bowling pin bowing pins and began to . . . juggle. Brad and Debra were astounded at the skill and mobility displayed by the ungainly Kogovsek. Despite the darkened room and the clutter that made ordinary walking difficult, the fat man danced and spun, performing amazing feats of dexterity until Brad forgot all about the gun and gave Mr. K a standing "O." Debra clapped half-heartedly.

"You know," Kogovsek said, bowing in appreciation of the recognition, his small audience afforded him, "I'll be needing a drummer."

*

"So how's Brad?" Sheila asked. "I haven't heard you say anything about him for a month or more.

"I don't know. Haven't seen him."

"So you finally got smart and dumped him."

"Not exactly. He moved out."

Sheila's expression said volumes.

"Just don't ask."

The Vortitron

"Hurry up, Hon. You're appointment with Dr. Chambers is in an hour."

"I just need to do a few more calculations," I say. "I want to run a quick test on the unit."

"Well, don't be long. I laid out your shirt and shoes next to your new jacket. And remember, we have to drive all the way across town. You know how the traffic is at this time of day."

New jacket. Traffic. I don't want to see Dr. Chambers. Why can't they just let me work? It's vital that I finish the Vortitron by January.

Oh hell. It's only been ten minutes. Here she comes again.

Jeanette's footsteps reverberate outside the laboratory door.

"You've got to stop now. You can work later. You have to shower and get dressed. Besides, you spend all your time down here in the basement lately. What is that thing anyway?"

"It's the Vortitron," I say, trying to control my anger. "And stop calling the laboratory 'the basement.'"

I'm shaking now.

"OK. OK I forgot. It's your laboratory." She pats my arm. "Now let's go."

She leads me by the elbow, out of the lab and up the steps. I look back at the machine on my workbench, still plugged into the power strip. Its little LED lights flicker occasionally as its hard-drive brain continuously assesses atmospheric and gravitational conditions. I'm stumped though. I can't seem to get the thing to overcome the differential in real distance between here and Mars considering the warping effect of gravity and speed.

On our way up the steps, I have to marvel at the miracle of the ivy vine that has worked its way through the tiniest crack around the basement window. Ivy leaves obscure the light, partially covering the exterior of the window. I reach out as we pass, absently brushing one of the leaves the vine has managed to insinuate into the interior. Not one living atom has been found anywhere other than on this planet, yet here, entire industries thrive in the production of tools to trim it, beat it back, pull it off, hunt it down, reel it in. We manufacture chemicals to limit its growth, to alter it, to suppress it, to eradicate it.

"The Vortitron," I explain to her as best I can in lay terms, "when working properly, will overcome the wave effect present in the visible spectrum. Once that is accomplished, I should be able to substitute infrared for violet—or purple as you call it."

"OK— well," she pats my arm again, "you get ready now. You can explain all that to Dr. Chambers."

"Dr.Chambers. Dr. Vincent. Those idiots from CNN, NBC, CBS. I'm sick of it all. Why can't they just let me do my job?"

"So, Mr. O'Ferrel," Chambers says, "how have you been doing since our last session?"

"Well, I'm making some progress but I've hit a sort of roadblock with the Vortitron's ability to differentiate between certain wavelengths of the visible spectrum. In theory, as you're probably aware, it should be able to take all the components of each individual color of light, separately mind you, and put them together to add up to white."

"I see," says the doctor, tapping his fingers together thoughtfully. "The Vortitron."

He looks at me over the top of his hateful little glasses. They're the kind of half-frames that intellectual types like to use for effect. He's not fooling me. He doesn't need those glasses.

"And so," I say. "I really need to land this grant, if I'm to finish the Vortitron by January, the next time Mars will be close enough."

"Yes, yes. Mars. The grant. Yes. Hmm."

I watch as he jots something down in his little book.

"So tell me, Mr. O'Ferrel, what do you remember about your experiences? You know, on Mars."

"Jesus! Do I have to go through it all again? Didn't anyone catch the CNN interview?"

"Well, actually, Mr. O'Ferrel, none of my staff has been able to come across a copy or a transcript of the interview you have spoken of."

"What about CBS? NBC?"

"Sorry."

Chambers gives me a sheepish, apologetic grimace.

"All right, all right for Christ's sake," I say. "One more time."

I try to get a grip. But I'm so tired of going over this again and again. I don't really want to relive it. I'm not in any way responsible for those deaths. If Lieutenant Harris, and Dr. Porter had checked the fuel cells before we set down they'd be alive today.

"Tell me again, what it was like. Did you see—anyone—talk to anyone—there?"

"You mean other than Porter and Harris?"

"Yes."

"Well, what do *you* think? After we landed, and the craft settled down, we cleared the envelopes from the scope. Of course we had no idea exactly what the terrain would be like until the ship came to a complete stop because we had rolled quite a ways past our intended landing site. You know, I mean after the bouncing subsided."

"Of course."

"The area we had chosen was relatively free of craters and obstructions but the weather in those latitudes can be fearful—high winds, sand storms. Harris and I were to take the rover and drilling rig to an area below a ridge about two miles from the module. Porter stayed with the lander where he maintained contact with Houston—and us. Then Harris and I started our dig. The drilling went relatively smoothly."

"The drilling?"

"Yes. But at first we had a hard time clearing the sand. It kept drifting back into the opening and we had to stop frequently to clean it out. After a few hours we managed about twenty feet into the crust. At the end of the first day, things were looking AOK. We drove the rover back to the ship for a decent night's sleep and a meal. You know how *that* is —have you tried the spaghetti? I like to twirl the tube around and pretend that I'm using a fork and spoon."

Chambers smiles and nods. I guess he's tried it too. He taps his fingers together. "Please, go on."

"When we returned the next day, the digging was much easier, but we didn't find water. The idea, of course, was that in this dry lake-bed we might find a pocket of subterranean water. But there was nothing. We collected samples of rock and did a cursory search for fossil evidence. No luck."

Chambers does not respond to this.

"But then we hit the jackpot. Man, Harris and I couldn't believe it."

"The inscription?" Chambers asks.

"I thought you didn't know about this," I say.

"Your wife told me, of course—about the inscription."

"We were leaving the excavation. We had to climb

out by way of an extension ladder. You know. We left the
drilling rig behind, the way we leave all the other junk on
Mars, the moon—wherever. That's when Harris grabs my
arm and points to the side of the pit. He's very excited.
Then I see it. Writing of some kind. Right there on the
rock. We must've broken through a kind of cave wall. I
did drawings of it. Look."

I show him my sketchbook, with my copy of what
I saw. It's on the same page with the watercolor I had done
the previous day. The illustration depicted the lander in its
position on the surface. I had been captivated by the con-
trast between the reddish and sepia landscape and the collapsed air cushions and polished metal of our craft.
Partially obscuring that image and continuing on to the
next page, is my careful transcription of what appeared to
be writing, as well as my copies of the pictographic dia-
grams of the machine, currently pulsating impatiently for
me back at my laboratory worktable.

"See," I say, "There's the date, on the top of the
page. I always date my drawings and watercolors. It helps
me remember just how things were. Look."

I leaf back about ten pages. "Here's a sketch I did
of the Duomo in Florence. I never carry a camera."

Chambers leafs through my book, lingering over
the drawings—hands it back to me.

"It got burned in the descent. I was lucky to save it
from the crash. Well hell. Truth is, I was just lucky— period. Harris and Porter died of dehydration before we made
it back. Oh, I know what they're all thinking. I know what
you're thinking."

Chambers face reveals nothing to me. If he
believes that I was hoarding supplies, he doesn't show it.

I see him raise his eyes to the glass panel on the
wall. I'm not fooled. It's some kind of signal to whoever is
watching from behind the fake mirror. Two men in white
enter the room. Chambers nods to them and they

approach.

"They're not pinning this on me," I say. "Harris and Porter were idiots. I warned them repeatedly about the fuel cells but they wouldn't listen. They just laughed at me. They wanted my book. But I slept with it right here."

I clasp the book to my chest.

"If they tried anything I was ready. But I didn't have to worry about them for long. They were weak. Only the strong survive. You know that, DOCTOR!"

"We have something here to relax you," he says, soothingly.

They've got my arms now and one of them is injecting something in my shoulder.

"No! No!"

But it's too late. I feel myself letting go. That's when I notice—none of them have NASA insignias.

"We're going to help you Mr. O'Ferrel. Your wife thinks that you should stay with us for a time . . .until you're feeling better."

I don't care now. I see the doctor and Jeannette talking. Now she's kissing me. She holds my book. I want to reach for it but my arms don't seem to belong to me anymore. I hear them talking. The voices sound hollow—far away.

"It'll take some time, Mrs. O'Ferrel. He thinks he's been on Mars. He's suffering from guilt over the deaths of these two imaginary figures. But—I think we should pick up this machine he's building. You've seen it right? It really exists?"

"Yes, Doctor. It's down in the basem . . .er his . . .laboratory."

"Good. We'll send someone over. It could pose a danger. You never know with someone in his . . .condition. Give it a couple weeks Mrs. O'Ferrel. With medication and therapy he'll be right as rain. Oh, and I'd better hang on to that."

Through a pleasant fog, I see the man take my book, but it's hard to care.

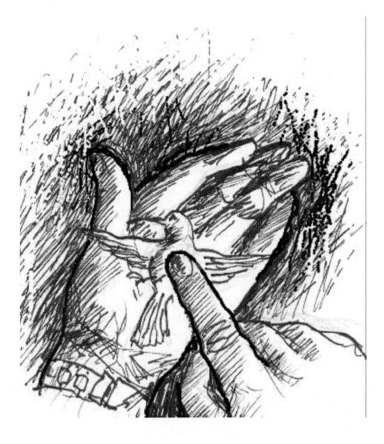

A Savior

Pete limped into the kitchen for a fresh cup of coffee. Mornings were tough sometimes, until his joints loosened up. He pried the lid off the Motrin and popped two of the little orange pills.

"What time do you expect them?" He asked.

He tried to project a matter-of-fact tone, offhandedly showing a cavalier indifference about the whole matter. It didn't really matter to him whether he saw his great nephew today, tomorrow, or next year.

"Well," Janie said, "Maggie said they'd try to get away around ten . . . so they ought to be here at about one if they stay on the interstate."

Pete dressed and ambled out to his workshop where he piddled with a few of the projects he had going. His belt sander had stopped tracking properly. It would be easy enough to get himself a new one for about thirty-five bucks down at the ACE, but he hated to give up on something that still had a few good years left in it, without even making an attempt at R & R. Nevertheless, as he fingered the forty odd parts of the disassembled tool, he found that he wasn't interested in taking up that task today. He ran his hand over the newly acquired sheen of the grandfather clock he had unearthed at a local yard sale. It worked but didn't keep accurate time. He knew little about clock mechanisms, but as he always said, "You can learn anything from a book." But even the ancient timepiece held little interest for him today.

He unwedged his basketball from between a gallon of paint thinner and some coffee cans filled with nuts and bolts. He bounced it a few times. Too much air. He let some out and bounced again. He had overdone it. He pumped some back until the bounce was exactly the same as it had been five minutes before. Perfect.

*

"Come on now, Jason. Get up. It's almost 10:30."

"Aw, Mom, It's Saturday. Lemme sleep."

"No, now get up. Remember, we're going to visit Uncle Pete and Aunt Janie."

"Why don't you go? Why do I have to go along? Me and Josh and Kinsey were going to play some soccer with these guys from Avondale."

"You know, Jason, Uncle Pete and Aunt Janie raised me. They want to see you now and then. You're like a grandson to them."

"But, Mom, you know how he is. He'll make me play pool, or ball, or wrestle. He . . . he's such a bully. I don't want to go."

"That's just his way. He was just like that with me growing up. You get used to it. And besides, you're a boy. You know, he always wanted a son. I was OK, but he could never quite mold me into his vision. Besides, Aunt Janie's making dinner and we need to get away from here for a while. It'll do us both good."

"Someday soon," she promised him, "we'll get our own house again . . . when I can get back on my feet."

In the three years since the "separation" she had to admit, the signs of getting back on her feet were not obvious. She scanned the tiny apartment, which sometimes closed in on her until she felt like a prisoner. The old car Uncle Pete had "loaned" her was still running . . . barely. She hoped it would survive this trip back to Pete and Janie's, perhaps to its final resting place. She had her eye on a new SUV and even though she dreaded the ordeal facing her, she had made up her mind to broach the subject with Pete. Heck, with zero percent financing, the new SUV would be cheaper than some used cars.

Jason dressed, considering the day ahead of him. At least the drive out to Aunt Janie's—away from the city, the noise, the traffic—always calmed him. He actually liked to be alone, unlike like his friends who had to be doing something exciting and expensive all the time. He loved to hike back into Uncle Pete's woods—without Uncle Pete, of course—without anyone, just to be alone and listen to the wind in the trees. He thought about the last time they were there. He had been able to escape from Uncle Pete and had gone off by himself. His foot's loud crunch had startled a coyote that leapt up five feet in front of him. The animal had simply materialized out of the ground. It must have been sleeping there in the heat of midday, waiting for dusk, to begin its rounds. There was something sad and familiar in the way it had looked back

at him with those wise yellow eyes before it bolted. It had
been like looking in a mirror.

*

When they pulled into the drive, Aunt Janie came
running down the steps to hug them both. His great uncle
stood on the porch, sipping coffee. Uncle Pete had been an
imposing figure for as long as Jason could remember, a
big man, with a huge head, broad shoulders and meathook
hands. Over the last two or three years he had put on a little weight around the middle, but he still looked powerful
and muscular.

But it wasn't just that. It was his big ways. Big
persona. Big talk. Loud talk. Lots of talk. And now, here
he came.

"Oh Janie, It feels so good here. It's so cool and
the air is so clean," said Maggie, twirling in the driveway.

"I know, Honey. I wish you two could move up
here."

"I gotta be where I can find work. There's nothing
for me here."

"Of course you're right, but that city is so imper-
sonal and hot. And, it's dangerous. I worry about Jason
growing up there. You know. You hear about all those
gangs and drugs."

"You don't have to worry about Jason. He's a good
boy and his friends are nice. They don't even like girls . .
.yet."

"What?" said Pete, slapping the boy on the back

with his heavy hand. "Where's that stick you carry, Son?"

"What stick, Uncle Pete?"

"The one you must have to use to fight those girls off with. Don't he look like he'd have to fight 'em off with a big ol' stick, Momma?"

With those words, Pete slapped a cough out of his nephew.

"How's your game comin', Son? You look like you could do some real damage in there."

Pete held the boy at arms' length, sizing him up.

Despite a softness in the boy's demeanor that was an affront to his uncle, Jason was already 6'3". And although he was thin, his nearly 200 pound frame was accentuated by considerable muscle.

"Hell, I bet when you set your mind to it, you can really take that ball to the hole," Pete said.

"I don't like basketball, Uncle Pete. I'm playing soccer for Matheson Senior."

"Soccer! Did you hear that, Momma?" Pete yelled toward his wife and Maggie.

"Here we go," Maggie said under her breath to Janie.

"Soccer's a sissy sport," Pete told Jason. "Come on out back and lemme give you a lesson or two in the real game."

"Pete!" Janie said. "Leave him alone. Come on in the house and be sociable."

Pete backed off and put his thick arm around the boy's shoulders, leading him toward the house. "Guess

we'll have to put that off a bit and go visit with the women
folk until they get tired of us."

As they walked up the steps, Pete gave a longing
glance down toward his basketball court. He was tired of
shooting around out there all by himself. He certainly did-
n't want to miss any opportunity to share his creation with
another athlete, willing or not. It wasn't a real full-court,
but as driveway basketball courts go, it was certainly top
of the line. When they had lived in town, he had put a goal
up on the garage. But the ball was always bouncing into
Janie's flowers or worse, into that bastard Clarence
Morgan's yard. Morgan was actually younger than Pete,
but Pete referred to him as Old Man Morgan.

That son of a bitch, he thought, *always calling the
cops over it, or just taking the ball and keeping it.*

So when Pete retired from his high school coaching job and bought his 35 acres, he pulled out all the stops.
He poured himself a regulation half-court concrete slab
and put in a professional-type goal— not one of those
cheap looking portable things with the big black plastic
base that you fill up with sand or water, then trip over and
bust your ass when you're driving in for a lay-up.

He stood admiring his creation. This baby was the
real McCoy, —official-looking as hell—steel post set in
concrete, offset glass backboard, with a heavy-duty break-
away rim (not that he was likely to be dunking).

His real pride and joy though, was the court itself.
He had poured the slab on different days in separate ten by
ten sections, painstakingly pressing into each one, hun-

dreds of imprints of a twelve inch by three inch piece of
maple flooring, to create a repeating pattern of interlock-
ing grid-work. For this tedious operation, he designed and
built a special rolling platform to suspend himself above
his malleable slab. The device consisted of a welded-steel
frame with a steel-mesh top. The contraption was
equipped with little railroad-type wheels that rolled along
a track he laid down on either side of the concrete section
he was working on.

He would kneel on the platform and as he worked,
roll himself along, "like *Porgy*" he had thought at the time,
humming *I Got Plenty O' Nothin'* while hovering above
the wet cement until the job was completed.

He remembered standing back and admiring his
handy-work after he had applied a golden stain-sealer to
the main areas, painted the lane and free-throw lines
green, and topped it all off with a picture, albeit crudely
done, of a leprechaun tipping his hat . . . back where the
center circle would be on a real court. Here at eighty-five-
hundred feet in the rarified air of the Colorado Rockies,
was a passable replica of the parquet floor of the old
Boston Garden.

Everybody who told him he'd miss coaching had
been right. But he sure didn't miss teaching drivers' ed.

Janie snapped him out of his reverie.

"What are you doing out there, Pete? Get in here."

*

She brought out a tray of snacks, coffee for Pete
and Maggie, a Coke for Jason and a teapot for herself.

"So how's school this year, Hon?" Janie asked Jason.

"Fine."

"Grades still good? You know, you have to keep them up if you want to get into a good college."

Jason munched on a cookie and said nothing.

"Man of few words," Pete observed.

"He's hoping to get a soccer scholarship," said Maggie.

"Hell," Pete said. "They don't give scholarships for soccer."

"Th . . . they do Uncle Pete," Jason replied. He glanced quickly at his mom to see if his impertinence had overstepped any boundaries.

Pete rolled his eyes, got up and went into the kitchen to pour more coffee.

The two women sent a silent signal to each other that neither Pete nor Jason detected.

"Pete," Janie said in her most soothing change-of-subject voice, "Maggie says she's looking at a new car."

"A new car!" Pete shouted back toward the living room. "What's wrong with that car I gave you?" He turned, sloshing his coffee as he hurried back toward the women and Jason. "Lemme take a look at it. It's probably something I can fix. Hell, these cars these days . . . everybody thinks that every time they sputter a little bit, it's *electronics*," he said, hissing the word, "or fuel injectors gone bad. Most of the time it's the same old stuff it's always been. Plugs or fuel filter or . . ."

"Pete! It's nothing like that. That old car is used up," Janie said. "It leaks when it rains and there's a whining noise from the engine."

"I didn't hear any whining noise."

"You can't hear."

"Probably just a belt slipping. I can spray some belt dressing on it."

"Isn't that the stuff you sprayed on your crotch by mistake, that time when you had jock itch?" Maggie asked.

The adults laughed, remembering this favorite tidbit of family history. Despite himself, a smile even crossed Jason's face, although he had heard the story before from his mom.

"Burned like hell." Pete said, smiling for the first time today. "I saw it come out of that can in a stream instead of a spray pattern. Felt like I was on fire. I thought, 'That's funny.' So I shook it up real good and sprayed again with exactly the same results. Then I read the label." He paused. "That reminds me — that spray pattern I was looking for is exactly the pattern a properly working fuel injector should produce."

The women looked at each other.

Janie turned to her husband.

"You have a God-given ability to destroy a mood," she said. "Anyway, Maggie's found this nice little SUV, — with zero percent financing, they're practically giving them away."

"Giving them away! Hell, they all cost twenty

grand nowadays."

The two women exchanged a glance, then dropped their gaze quickly back to their drinks.

"Well," Janie said, "I don't want Maggie and Jason driving around in that old junker any more. I think this is a good idea, and I'm going to help her out a little."

Pete made a sort of chuffing, grizzly bear noise.

"She ought to keep that "old junker" until she gets out of that thirty-thousand dollar credit card debt."

"You know Brian ran those cards up and left us holding the bag before he . . . before he left, Uncle Pete," Maggie said.

"Where is that bum now anyway? He out of jail yet?"

"Pete!"

Janie gave him a stern look and cut her eyes in Jason's direction.

"Excuse me please," Jason said. He got up and walked out the front door.

"Now see what you've done," Janie whispered, leaning toward Pete. "That's still his daddy you're talking about. Now you get out there and make up with him."

Pete walked out on the deck and watched his nephew scramble down the gully and up the other side, disappearing into the aspens. He figured he would be heading for the rocky outcroppings over the hill that offered a spectacular view of Mt. Princeton. The rocks were perched above the little creek that in some seasons chuckled with water as it played over the stones of its bed.

Of course, it would be dry now, but still, it was a spot that any visitor to his property would be drawn to.

He decided that he would give the boy a little time, sauntering slowly down the path Jason had taken, hands in pockets. He allowed himself calculated slides over the loose, rotten granite, letting gravity do some of the work meant for his aching knees and using his slow progress to work up something to say. Still, he had no intention of apologizing to the boy for any remarks regarding that no good, meth-amphetiine-using ne'r-do-well, cradle-robbing father of his. The last time he had laid eyes on the bum, he had been reminded of Keith Richard.

"How ya doin?"

Jason looked up, showing no surprise that his aunt had sent the old man to make amends.

"I'm OK," he said.

Pete sat down on a rock a respectable six or seven feet away.

"So," Pete ventured, "that old car been givin' y'all fits?"

"Nah. It's OK. It always starts at least. I guess Mom just figures it might not make another winter."

"Hmm."

Pete thought better of going down that road again, especially after chasing all the way out here. 'Course, if it was his car, which technically it was, since she refused to buy it off him at the reasonable price of one US dollar, he'd fix it up.

Janie was paying the insurance on it as their sec-

ond car because Maggie couldn't afford to pay the premi-
um. But he intended to offer to fix 'er up mechanically,
put on a new set of tires, work on those leaky window gas-
kets . . . hell, maybe even get a new windshield. Might
even sand 'er down and Bondo the dents and repaint 'er.
That baby'd pass for new by the time he finished. But he
knew, Maggie and Janie would still complain that it uses
too much gas. The newer cars were much more fuel effi-
cient, true. But hell, you could buy a lot of gas for twenty
thousand bucks.

Thoughtfully, he threw a rock at a Ponderosa on
the opposite side of the dry stream-bed. It resounded with
a satisfying *crack* as it curved in to strike the trunk dead
center. The sound reverberated through the stillness of the
woods.

"So," Pete tried again, "You really *don't* have a
girlfriend?"

"Well, actually there is this girl . . . Madison."

"Madison! That's a girl's name? Sounds like a
street, or a shortstop for the Yankees. She a real looker?"

Jason appeared to consider this.

"Well, I guess she is sort of pretty. But the main
thing is, she's real smart and funny. She likes outdoor
stuff. She's kinda different from the other girls I know. I
don't think she's real popular."

"Smart huh? Well I guess a girl named after a president oughta be smart."

"She'd really like it here. She's a year ahead of me.
She . . . she's got her license. Do you . . . do you think it'd

be OK if the two of us came up here some weekend, you
know . . . to go hiking and stuff . . . just for the day?"

"Well sure . . . be glad to have you. Spend the
weekend. Jefferson can stay in the upstairs bedroom and
you can have the cot in the family room down in the basement. We don't want no funny business," Pete said with a
wink.

Jason smiled back.

"It's Madison," he said. But he knew his uncle was
joking now.

"Whatever." Pete said. "If she's as smart as you
say, I bet she'd like a little Trivial Pursuit. We'll play boys
against girls."

"I don't know . . ."

"We can work the details out when she gets here,"
Pete said, rubbing his hands in anticipation of the new
challenge. "You and me can kick a little butt."

They sat quietly for a few minutes.

Pete noticed a movement to his right and signaled
silently to Jason. A big brown fox with a bush of a tail,
nearly as long as its body, wandered into the scene. The
fox was upwind. It never noticed them as it sniffed around
the trees and pawed at the pine needles, passing within
feet before disappearing over the hill.

"Anyway," Pete resumed, "the women folk are
gonna be havin' dinner ready soon. What say we go work
up a good appetite?"

Jason understood that this was the dreaded invitation to play basketball. But considering his uncle's gra-

ciousness regarding Madison, he felt he couldn't refuse.

"OK, let's play a game of HORSE," Jason offered.

*

"It looks like they're getting along pretty well," Maggie observed, seeing them come up the hill together.

"Now don't you boys get all sweaty and nasty," Janie yelled from the door, when she saw Pete pick up the ball and toss it to Jason. "We're going to eat in about a half hour."

"It's alright," Pete shouted back toward the house. "We're just playin' a little game of HORSE."

They finished the game, which Pete won H to H-O-R-S-E.

"Let's go in, Uncle Pete."

"Aw come on, Boy. That wasn't enough to even earn me a French-Fry."

He patted his slight paunch.

"I don't like to eat until I've earned my supper. How 'bout a game to twelve straight, by ones and twos, make it-take it, your ball first."

When Jason signified his agreement to this plan by not refusing, Pete jogged over to the car to retrieve his knee braces and other gear required for the business at hand. He had long ago worn out the sixty-dollar brace pre-scribed to him by the surgeon who had repaired his left knee twice and his right knee once. These were from Wal-Mart. Seventeen ninety-five a pop. He had gone through twelve of them already. The sweat rotted away the threads that held the Velcro fasteners after about six months of daily use in his regular noontime game down at the Y. He kept his mid-day appointment as if it were his job, despite the hour drive each way.

"Here we go," said Janie to Maggie, nudging her and pointing to the car where Pete was bent to his task of what he called "girding his loins for battle."

On his left knee he wore only one brace, mostly as a precaution. But on his right, the one that was permanently swollen, the one he was supposed to ice down two times a day, he wore two, strapped over each other as tightly as he could cinch them. Ever since his back surgery, six or seven years ago, he had played while wearing a back brace— the kind the stock boys at the lumber-yard were required by law to wear—except not wanting to look completely ridiculous, he had cut the shoulder straps away from his. The goggles had been a regular part of his uniform, since his fourth visit to the emergency room for the same eye injury had at last taught him that lesson. The elbow and wrist braces were just for minor annoyances.

"You need to stop this," Janie had told him when she saw him rubbing liniment on his swollen elbow just last week. "Your not a kid any more."

"Hell, It's nothin'. You don't have to walk on your elbow."

He smiled to himself now, thinking about Cindy, who ran track for the local college. She used to be one of his driver's-ed students. She made fun of his uniform when he came out of the locker room. She often waited outside the locker room door at noon for the guys she ran with while he and his bunch played ball. Sometimes when he passed by her, encased in all his bindings, she would bang into him with that hard little ass of hers before giving him her opinion of his chosen game.

"Basketball is a pussy sport."

Maggie watched from the kitchen window as he lumbered stiffly from the car back to the court, wrapped in multiple bandages, resembling a less benign version of the Michelin Tire man.

Pete won the first game, twelve-two.

"You can do better than that," he chided Jason. "You're not trying. When you drive to the basket, use your body to establish your position."

"We're ready to eat!" Maggie shouted from the doorway.

"One more game," came Pete's reply.

"Look at them out there," Maggie said to Janie. "Now they're sweaty, especially Pete. He's wringing wet."

"They can clean up pretty quickly," Janie said. "Jason can change into one of Pete's T-shirts. We'll let them finish this game."

"When you rebound the ball," Pete said, "keep your arms up and pivot into your man." Pete demonstrated this maneuver by turning into the boy and thrusting his rear into Jason's gut causing him to let out an "oomph" and double over in pain. "Like Kevin McHale."

"Who's Kevin McHale?" Jason asked, wincing.

"Never mind. Just tee it up, Son."

Jason drove toward the basket and threw up a weak

attempt as he bounced off his uncle. The ball glanced
harmlessly off the underside of the rim.

"Bring it into me strong . . .not like some pansy.
Like this."

He swung his elbow into the kid's jaw, knocking
him to the faux parquet.

"That's enough now, boys. It's time to get cleaned
up," Janie called.

Jason picked himself up and started toward the
house.

"Where do you think you're going?" Pete said.
"We're not quite though here."

Jason looked at him but said nothing, resuming his
progress toward the house.

Pete grabbed the boy's arm with enough force that
Jason grimaced in pain, looking down at the arm. He
shook free of Pete's iron grip.

"Alright," Jason said, lets finish it. "What's the
score?

Pete noticed a definite trace of anger in the boy's
tone.

"Seven-five, my way," Pete said, smirking. "Win
by two." He could see competiveness replace the former
laid-back demeanor in his great nephew. "Soccer," he said,
"Hmmph."

Jason caught up and the game went back and forth
for a while. The boy was now using his nearly two hundred pounds and three-inch height advantage to take the
game to his uncle. They reached the scoring objective of

twelve points, tied. Needing an advantage of two points to claim victory, the game was essentially in overtime.

"Extra innings," Pete said. "Crunch time. Let's see what ya got left in the tank, Boyo."

Pete scored from out.

Jason took it up and under.

Sixteen – sixteen. Pete was beginning to feel the age difference. Maybe soccer had put the kid in pretty good shape after all.

"Jason! Pete! Get your butts in here."

It was Maggie.

"I just need two more points, Mom. I got the old man on the ropes here."

Jason drove the lane and Pete, thinking he could lunge through Jason's mid-section for a steal, caught one of the sixteen-year-old's fat-free, razor-sharp elbows in the mouth as the boy protected the ball in the manner his uncle had so recently recommended. Pete was staggered. He glanced at Jason, moving only his eyes above the hand that covered his painful, bleeding lip.

Seventeen – sixteen — Jason.

Pete took the ball. He faked right then started his move to the left. Jason didn't fall for the fake. He hung right with him, and when Pete spun back the other way to try one of his patented hook shots, which usually worked, even against taller, younger and more athletic players, Jason smacked it with the efficiency of a flyswatter against a gnat, causing the ball to ricochet painfully off Pete's nose.

Jason chuckled. When he made his next move to the basket, Pete buckled in pain as something popped in his left knee — the good one.

"You OK?" Jason asked.

"It's nothing," Pete snapped. "Just gimme a second."

"We can quit. You're hurt. Let's go eat."

"I'm fine. I just need to shake it off."

He repeatedly flexed his knee and heard a popping sound from somewhere deep inside, not the usual popping sound.

Pete took the ball again and drove, this time, no fake. He powered into Jason's midsection and when the boy reeled backward, he started to go up with his shot. But before he could really gather himself, Jason had recovered and it became clear to Pete that his shot would be rejected once more. Out of frustration, he gave an arm fake. The intent of this move with this free arm was to get his opponent to react as if it were a scoring threat. But Jason didn't react and Pete's heavy and powerful left elbow caught the boy on the right cheekbone where the thin layers of muscle and flesh are closest to the bone. The neat one and a half inch gash that opened there was so perfect that it could have been the incision of a surgeon's carefully wielded scalpel.

By the time Maggie and Janie got out to the driveway to check on him, his eyes were rolled back in his head and blood flowed copiously from the wound.

"He'll be fine," Pete said. "Go get some water and

ice."

Janie came back with water, and the women tended to him until, in just a few minutes, he opened his eyes. Janie closed the wound as best she could with two over-sized Band-Aids.

Pete held up two fingers.

"Two."

"Who's the President?"

Jason correctly named the individual currently residing in the Oval Office. In an effort to lighten the mood, Pete asked him to identify the Vice President. Neither Jason, nor the two women could quickly come up with the answer. They all laughed.

"I was ahead, when the game ended. So I win," Jason said groggily, as they helped him to his feet.

"I think we should take him in to the clinic," Janie said. "They ought to check him for a concussion."

"I'll get his jacket," said his mother.

"Game's not over," Pete said, "If there's not a con-cussion, we'll finish it when you get back."

They all stared at him.

"What?"

*

Pete watched the dust cloud dissipate in the wake of the car carrying the little family group down the dirt and gravel county road toward the clinic. He went into the house where the food sat untouched on the table. He tore off a chunk of turkey and popped it into his mouth. He went to the fridge and pulled out a can of Coors Light and cracked it open.

He sat down and draped his ice bag over his right knee and flipped on the NBA Eastern Finals game. He took a swig of beer. Who were these bums? No Boston. No New York Knicks. Toronto — New Orleans. Who cared?

A loud thump attracted his attention from the game. He looked out toward the deck and at first saw nothing. Then he noticed something sticking up from between the cracks in the decking. A piece of wood? No. Upon closer examination, he realized it was the tail of a humming bird. It must have flown into one of the enormous picture windows. He had feared, at the time he designed the house that the oversized windows would present a problem in the late afternoon when the sun beamed through—and he was right. They had tried to live with them during that first summer, but in the end had been forced to trade in some beauty for comfort by installing a darkened, mirrored film, reducing the heat by 90 percent. Unfortunately, birds now saw the huge mirrors as a continuation of the open sky, and flew into them with alarming, fatal frequency. This one however, was not quite dead.

He held the tiny creature carefully in his big right hand and gently stroked the bird's beautiful iridescent breast. It was completely limp and unconscious, but breathing. As he turned his hand, the opalescent colors at its throat shifted from red to green in the changing light. He placed the animal gently on the boards of the deck in the fading sunlight and went back into the house, returning shortly with a bowl of cold water and a towel. He picked up the bird carefully and laid it on the folded towel. Like a priest sprinkling holy water, he repeatedly drizzled moisture on the little bird, in an effort to revive it. At last he abandoned this seemingly fruitless campaign and returned to his game.

Every few minutes he looked out to see that the bird was still there. At halftime he went back out and sprinkled more water on it. He picked it up again. Dead? But just as he was about to toss it over the deck railing, it opened its tiny eyes. Still on its back, it lay there in his hand, panting and groggily examining its strange savior, not aware that this same huge creature had been the cause of its crisis in the first place. With amazing agility it righted itself and flew out of Pete's hand, returning to hover in front of him for a few seconds, as if acknowledging his kindness, before flying away toward the mountains.

Just then the car rounded the curve in the road. They had been gone for hours. For a little scratch like that? Not wanting to appear concerned, he dashed back in the house to grab his beer in order to make a show of casually sipping it. As the car approached he could see that it contained three upright passengers. When they got out he noticed the bandage covering the wound on Jason's temple.

"Seven stitches. No concussion," was Janie's verdict as they walked up the steps to the deck.

"Ready to finish the game?" Pete asked his great-nephew before taking a pull from his beer.

"No thanks, Uncle Pete. I think I'll just concede this one."

Pete made a fist and drew his bent arm toward his body in a gesture similar to the one he used to give to truckers as a boy, to be rewarded with a blast of the air horn—a gesture that said Y-E-S.

"But," Jason added, "When I come back with Madison, we'll play best of seven."

Pete smiled . . . He had him.

56th Street

Damn! These laptops are supposed to be so thin —
and light. I'm gonna be sweaty by the time I get there.
What am I going to say anyway? I should have given this
more thought.

"Welcome to the future of telecommunications.
No, too boring. Ladies and gentlemen, the future is now
— no — the future is . . ."

Oh shit, a homeless guy. Don't make eye contact.

"The future of telecommunica . . ."

Aw man . . . he's nailed me. How do they know? I
must have *out-of-towner* stamped across my forehead.
What have I got here . . . feels like nickels . . . dimes . . .
wait a minute . . . here's a buck.

"Here ya go buddy."

"Ladies and Gentlemen, wel . . ."

"What the fuck is this?" the guy shouts. He looks
at the bill in his hand like it's a three-day-old ham sand-
wich, which, by the looks of the guy, shouldn't be a problem anyway.

Walk on. Straight ahead. No eye contact. Just stay
focused on the woman in the black raincoat, the one just
behind all those other people in black raincoats. Shit. He's
got my arm.

"What the fuck *is* this?" the bum shouts again. "a fuckin dollar? Here Mac. I can't do nothin with this. I NEED TEN BUCKS you cheap son of a bitch! . . . Fuckin dollar," he mutters.

He throws the dollar down and spits on the sidewalk at my feet. Walking ahead of me — backwards, he keeps his eyes fixed on mine. My own eyes remain locked on the black raincoat, or at least *a* black raincoat. Something in me, something so *cheap*, makes me yearn for the dollar. Don't think about it. But . . .I hate to throw money away.

Can't go back now; he's watching me. Somebody's picked it up by now anyway.

"I want my ten bucks you shit!" the beggar shouts at me. The guy just won't let this go.

"Shut up. Leave me alone. I gave you money. Now fuck off. I've got a meeting."

"A meeting!" he shouts. "I got a meeting too. It'll cost me twenty bucks to attend and I'm ten short. Now gimme that ten."

What the hell is going on here? Doesn't anybody see this? Don't they care? I stop. His eyes dart from mine to my hand and back as I pull out my wallet and extract the ten. What the hell? It'll be worth it to get rid of him. I've lost the woman in the black raincoat.

"Here! Take it. Now get lost."

He takes the bill, pockets it and starts to walk away — to leave me in peace. But no. He turns back.

"Charlie?" he says. "Charlie Merchant? Harrison

High – '81?'"

I don't say anything. I slowly resume my progress toward 56th keeping my gaze fixed resolutely forward.

"Ned — Ned Hass, remember? You used to post up in the middle and I'd cut through and rub my man off your screen. But you never could catch my return pass after you rolled off the pick." He laughs.

I smile now remembering how I never could get the hang of that play no matter how many times we ran it. I could set the pick but I couldn't roll off the screen and still catch the ball, so I usually just stopped where I had set my pick and Ned would throw the ball to the spot where I should have been.

"Why did you do it Ned?" I say. "I must have told you a hundred times I can't roll off those picks."

He laughs again and puts a finger to his left nostril and blows, expelling a copious stream of snot onto the street. "Hey man, thanks for the ten. I was just shittin' you about the meeting. You know how it is."

I jump back a bit to avoid the splatter as he shakes mucous from his blowing hand.

"So," I say, "How'd you . . ."

"How'd I wind up a homeless bum?"

"N . . no . . . I . . .How'd you end up in New York? It's a long way from Indiana."

"*You're* here," he says with a little laugh.

I'm very uncomfortable watching all the passers-by, having to work their way around our little class reunion. Ashamed of my discomfort, I feel my face turn-

ing red. I'm ashamed to be ashamed. Here's my old teammate. Maybe he *is* a little down on his luck but, . . .

"Listen," he says, "lemme show you somethin'."

"But . . .I have to get to this me..."

"Aw come on. They can wait a few minutes."

"Well, OK," I say.

Ned leads me around the corner and down an alley,
past overflowing dumpsters and blowing trash. We pass
through a portal whose detached metal door rests against
the adjacent wall. The hinges are still attached to the rust-
ing doorframe. We start down a set of clanging metal
steps. Cold fluorescent lighting soon gives way to darkness as we descend into the depths of the city, three, four,
five stories down. The sounds from the busy street disappear. We're left only with the occasional noise and vibra-
tion of a subway train, somewhere on the other side of the
wall to which the steps are anchored. It's pitch black now,
except for the occasional bare 60-watt bulb. I look up. Far
above, I can still see daylight from the open doorway.

"Listen Ned, I . . ."

"Come on, it's not much further now."

He gives me his brightest missing-toothed smile.

At last we arrive at the dark, smelly basement of
the subterranean city. As my eyes adjust to the darkness I
can see little pools of dim light from single bulbs off in
the distance. Ceilings of varying height loom above our
heads, supported by rusty I-beams. The stench of urine
and vomit is overwhelming and I'm sure I hear the scurry-
ing and squeaking of rats.

Ned calls out: "Hey grubs, I got one!"

I don't like the sound of this invitation and begin to move toward the stairs. I can think of nothing more appealing at this moment than the dismal alleyway overhead, with its stinking, overfilled dumpsters. But Ned grabs my arm, albeit gently, and gives me a grin. He puts his other hand on my back and gently coaxes me back to where we had been standing. Shadowy figures begin scuttling toward me from behind posts and partitions. I hear occasional splashes and their hollow, echoing footscrapings.

The ugliest woman I've ever seen approaches me with a cocked, inquisitive expression. I don't often find people to be truly ugly. If I look long enough, I can usually pick out some individual feature that has the effect of mollifying the collective ugliness of the whole, but not in this case. The absurd nose — bulbous and dripping — perfectly complements the bulging, leaky reddish eyeballs. The few pointed and snaggled teeth that remain in her head, protrude from a half missing lower jaw.

"Looky what I found Cindy," Ned says to the creature. "Watcha' think of this here?"

"Well I be," Cindy says.

She screws up her hideous face and brings her foul, fish-breath close enough to mine that I have to fight back my retch response.

"If it ain't Charlie Merchant."

I continue to stare, puzzled, as Ned smiles proudly at the little homecoming scene he has engineered.

"Cindy," she tells me. "Cindy Traylor. Remember?"

In order to jog my faulty memory, she grasps the ragged wisps of gray hair that protrude from her grimy stocking cap. With her other hand she tugs at her chin, stretching her face into a cucumber, as if the resulting ridiculous elongation will paint for me a recognizable portrait.

"Mr. Gwaltney's home room, third row, fourth desk. I guess you never paid me much mind," she caws, "I wasn't *popular* like ol' Ned here."

Her cackle is matched by Ned's viscous laugh as he hocks up a big lungwad and expels it expertly toward a cardboard box on which someone, probably Ned, has drawn a target, streaked with runny matter of all sorts.

"Yes," I say. "Yes I do remember you now. You had a friend — long blond hair — Sally, Sally Furgeson. Whatever happened to her?"

"Tumor," Cindy croaks. "Great big ol' tumor."

"I . . I'm sorry."

At that moment we're all startled to hear a sound from my inside coat pocket. My cell phone. I'm surprised, to say the least, that it works down in this hellish underworld as I pull it from my pocket. But before I can answer the call, Cindy snatches the thing from my hand with amazing speed and dexterity. As soon as she has it in her grasp she slams it into her forehead repeatedly until it cracks open and the little tune it plays to alert me of a call, the four fateful opening tones of Beethoven's Fifth, are

silenced. She hands the smashed communicator to Ned
who without hesitation tosses the phone into a pile of similar instruments at the base of one of the I-beams posts.

As if some kind of response is triggered by the
phone incident, the other figures, who until now have
stayed back in the gloom at a respectable distance, begin
to shuffle forward. I feel helpless and resigned to a fate
that I cannot imagine as the throng begins to fondle and
probe me with their dirty fingers. They remove my jacket,
shirt, trousers, shoes . . .everything. They relieve me of my
briefcase containing the laptop and my notes.

"Wait," I say.

"Shut up, turd," Ned says, giving me a little shove.
"Cid," Ned calls out to a figure about my size, dressed like
all the others in rags.

The man approaches. Ned hands him my clothing
and equipment. Cid strips off his own stinking garments
and presents them to my former teammate who in turn
passes them to me. I watch as the man puts on my clothing
and takes up my equipment.

"Where's your meeting?" Ned asks me.

"Uh, the Stronheim Group, 1257 W 56th Street."

Ned gives Cid a nod and a pat on the back, and the
man, now in my clothing, starts toward the metal stairway
and the distant light. But Ned calls him back. "Better take
this."

Ned takes a few bills out of my wallet, handed to
him by one of his droogies. He pockets the cash, then
passes the wallet and the remainder of its contents to Cid.

I notice as Cid walks away, how attractive he looks
in my outfit. If anything, he seems more confident than I. I
hear him muttering to himself, "Welcome Ladies and
Gentlemen. Welcome to the future."

Reluctantly I begin dressing in the foul-smelling
rags that recently cloaked Cid's form. The crotch area
feels wet. Once again I struggle against my gag response.
But in a few minutes I realize that I am actually relieved
to be rid of the burden of the suit, the laptop, the pressure
of my upcoming presentation. Everything seems easier
down here.

"Cindy will show you to your carton," says Ned,
patting me on the back. "Tomorrow you'll be assigned to
your area, but for now, why don't you get some rest."

I follow Cindy to an empty cardboard box. Inside
the box are some sheets of plastic bubble wrap, some
newspapers and a half empty bottle of Mad Dog 20-20.
Cindy gives me a gentle nudge toward my carton and kisses me lightly on the lips. Her non-functioning lower jaw
leaves a sodden trail on my face. I crawl in and settle
down, to the accompaniment of a few popping bubbles. I
pull the newspapers over myself and immediately feel at
peace.

"Charlie," says Cindy before walking off into the
gloom.

"Yes?"

"You really ought to drop a few pounds . . . you little shit."

I take a sip of the wine and consider her advice.

Summit Day

Outside my tent, the bustle of camp dies down for the night—only the hushed voices of the few Sherpas who talk quietly amongst themselves—and the sounds of a card game in progress in the communications tent disturb the stillness. I'd like to get some sleep, but it's always a problem for me here. My best bet is to read myself to sleep, but I've already read everything I packed along.

I hate the stuff the others read—Peter and his science fiction—or Greg, the leader—he's always reading accounts of other climbs. I don't want to read any more about that. Ang Lhakpa, Pertemba . . . none of the Sherpas have anything.

Out of desperation, I borrowed a paperback—something thin and lightweight— a volume entitled *Absolved,* by one Kenton Borden, who according to the author notes, lives, writes and fly-fishes in Kalispell, Montana.

My colleagues back at *Smathers, Black and Smathers*, have a totally romantic view of my activities here. They understand the physical stress, the pain and the occasionally fearsome weather, as well as the intrinsic rewards; I'm grateful that none of them ever ask me, "Why do it?"

They always seem willing to cover for me without complaining when I'm gone for months at a time. They don't say anything to my face at least. Right now, I guess Linda must be working on that malpractice suit with my *LynnCare* account.

Still— I've never been able to get across to them,

the days of tedium, of one foot in front of the other—basically a pack animal—hauling equipment and consumables for hours upon hours past the same sights you passed yesterday and the day before that. Humping loads up the fixed ropes and aluminum bridges of the icefall, or trapped for days in your tent by the weather, accomplishing nothing. Sometimes, the only relief from the boredom is the piss-your-pants fear each time you negotiate the alleyway between the ever-shifting seracs of the ice-fall, and you notice that one of the blue-white frozen condominiums is leaning six degrees more than when you last scuttled beneath it. Then—when you come back down from camp one the next day—it's gone—having been replaced by a new one, like a shark's tooth. Of course, we all understand that a stroll through the icefall is basically a game of Russian roulette. Run that gauntlet enough times and eventually that solitary bullet is going to nail you.

Sometimes I have to remind myself to appreciate my magnificent surroundings. Just before settling down with my book, I take a leisurely piss in the snow and make a point of admiring the spectacular sunset. The orange glow surrounding the countless snow peaks dissolves to a deep blue-going-black, dotted with the first of millions of stars. Stars at this altitude don't even twinkle. In this thin air they glow like steady little beacons.

I begin reading the Borden book, after a tasty dinner of freeze-dried Louisiana red beans and rice. Steve Sheldon, who is by now probably asleep in his own tent, was kind enough to cook. After much trouble with the tiny butane stove and the wearisome task of melting snow, a job, which at this altitude requires twice the time as it would back home, the meal was delicious. In return, it's my job to do the dishes.

Me, I have trouble with the altitude. It can do funny, or actually not so funny things to you. There's the nasty business of pulmonary or cerebral edema of course, or the plain misery of ordinary altitude sickness: headaches, nausea or the racking high-altitude cough. In my case, I can't sleep. Steve can sleep through anything: storms, pain, cold. Not me. If I get tired enough I might collapse into a coma-like state for an hour or so, but that's usually it.

So reading is fundamental.

I snuggle back in my bag, still in my full parka. It's a mild 10 degrees right now but likely to drop to 15 below with the clear night.

I skip over the introduction. Sometimes, if I find that I am engrossed, I will go back to read the intro. But I dive straight into the first chapter. The protagonist, Brian Edwards, and his family—wife Jennifer, kids Cara, 4 and Brandon, 6 are exploring the sub-alpine lake country of the Absorokas. The weekend trip is recreational, but we discover that Brian's love of the outdoors also supports his family. Much of his time as a writer of field guides and occasionally serious philosophical musings takes him on solo adventures into the ever-shrinking wilderness of the American West. By the time I reach chapter 4, I am familiar with the day-to-day domestic routine of their lives.

In chapters 5 and 6 we travel with him on one of his field outings, this one into the Wind River Range of northwestern Wyoming, in which he records his observations according to the example of John Muir. He also shows great patience in his photographic method, waiting for just the right light, following the advice of his other great mentor, Ansel Adams.

I sat on that uncomfortable rock from the time I discovered the view, already dazzling, even in the flat light of midday, until the long shadows of evening's amber light illuminated the rock faces and snow fields like a Thomas Moran canvas. After all that time and patience, I missed the photo of my life. I had just put my large format camera and tripod back in their cases, when I detected a move-

*ment. Ordinarily I would have been frightened at the sight
of a mother grizzly and her two cubs, but they were
upwind of me and were obviously so engrossed in their
activity, that mom was not checking as carefully as she
usually would for threats. The greatest threat to her cubs
would be a male grizzly, even the father of the two cubs.*

*They were quite obviously involved in pure play—a
game that had no more practical application than children
riding inner tubes down a snowy hill. The sow would
trudge her way up the snow slope with the kids following
rambunctiously behind, repeatedly giving them sled-rides
down the hill. The cubs rode by hanging onto her chest
while she made herself into a sled, sliding along on her
back while grasping her toes. They did this over and over
again until at last, even I had had enough and slipped
away without ever being observed.*

Outside the tent everything is quiet, as base camp
has put itself to bed, all except the glow of the lamp inside
my tent. The book seems to have taken a different turn in
the next chapter, in which Brian has accepted an offer to
read at a small midwestern college.

*I get some of my best thinking done in the car.
That's why, when I agreed to the honorarium at Southwest
Iowa College, I turned down their offer to fly me out. It
should only be two days by car, but once I've descended
the winding mountain roads of my home in western
Montana I can make good time on the straight, rural high-
ways, while enjoying the as yet unspoiled beauty of the
prairie, the eroded badlands and empty spaces of eastern
Montana and western North Dakota. I even enjoy what
would be to most folks—boring Iowa—without ever set-
ting rubber to interstate. What's an extra day?*

*My book: "Thirteen Days on the Salmon" is the
newest in my series of Zen-like guides to hiking, fishing
and canoeing— philosophical and physiological wander-
ings. The book describes a solo backpacking adventure*

into the winter stillness of the wilds, or at least what used to be the wilds, of the Bitterroots and the Frank Church Wilderness of Idaho. It's filled with complaints about and indictments of mining companies, logging enterprises, snow-mobilers, the forestry service, ranchers, oil men and all their Republican enablers: just the kind of work that I would expect to be given a sympathetic ear from a liberal institution like Southwest Iowa College.

Traveling through North Dakota, I am so taken with its cleanliness, that I am thinking of researching its history and people for a book. Heck, you could write a paragraph on every man, woman and child in the state and have only a moderate length book.

I know what to expect when I get to Southwest Iowa. The chair of the department—Laskowsky—I think his name was, will drive me around campus, pointing out this building, named for some dead alum who donated so many millions, or the new stadium, named for the living legend-recently-retired- soon to die of boredom and inactivity after forty years on the job that he would have stretched to fifty had not the fans, alums and board of regents been eager to see a more up to date "West-Coast offense". Then he'll take me to the only descent restaurant in town and drink heavily while he tells me how he never managed to publish that book he's been working on for twenty years because his "vision" for his department has kept him focused on the difficult task of bringing enlightenment to the local farm kids, but that when he retires three years from now, he will at last resume work on his novel and many other projects he has had to put on the back burner 'so to speak'.

When I arrived in town, it was not at all difficult to locate the campus, as signs proudly pointed the way. I stopped first at McDonalds for a cup of their vastly underrated coffee.

I found Laskowsky's office and introduced myself

to the secretary who sent me in.
"Professor Laskowsky? Brian Edwards."
He came around his desk to shake my hand.
"Nice to meet you Brian. I've read two of your
books and we're very excited to have you with us."
After driving me around town and pointing out the
various buildings named for dead alums, he took me to
lunch at the only decent restaurant in town, where he
ordered lots of drinks and told me about, among other
things, his book that he will someday finish, and the old
coach who has been forced out of his job.

I dread looking at my watch. I'm hoping for 3:30
AM but it's only 1:27. These sleepless nights seem to go
on forever. Reluctantly I extract myself from my bag and
unzip the tent flap to stand in the biting cold and pee in
the snow. In the crystalline night, I can see as well as if I
were standing in a city parking lot. The light from the stars
and the sliver of moon reflect from the snow. The other
peaks of the endless range nullify the starry matrix with
their pointy shapes.

I return to my bag and my book. By the light of my
little headlamp I follow the progress of Mr. Borden's protagonist from lunch with the professor, to his introduction
to the lecture hall where he will read from his new book,
sign his previous works and schmooze. At last, I feel the
tug of sleep.

*

"Hey man, Let's get a move on."
"Wha!" I awake, startled. "Wha . . .what time is
it?"

Steve's giant insect head—parka'd and goggle-
eyed—poking though my tent door, wakes me from a dis-
turbing dream to a not-enough-sleep-pre-dawn cold reality.
"It's four thirty. Gotta get up."
"Right," I say. I realize that I'm half sobbing from
my dream—another reason *not* to sleep. In the dream I'm

fighting with a neighbor who is intent on cutting down my 100-year-old piñons. All I have with which to discourage his work crew is a giant tongue depressor.

Two days from now, two members of our team, perhaps even Steve and I, will make the first summit bid. Today we're to go up to 25,000 ft. where we will set up camp four. We're not spending the night there. After we set up, we are to come all the way down to C-3 to breathe in a few more O's in order to help rebuild cells and strength we lose up there. It's up to Greg, our leader then. I will either return to C-4 with Steve to make the summit bid or go down to base and take up a support role. We've all agreed that we will do what it takes—no whining.

Steve leads under the crisp light of the full moon I can follow his progress up the Dutch Rib, as if it were day. The beam of his headlamp bounces unnecessarily across the snow slope ahead of him. I decide not to use mine. I can see perfectly in the ambient starlight—besides, I'm intent on enjoying the unreal clarity of the universe that so few are privileged to witness.

"Turn on your damned lamp!" he yells back to me.

Universe or not, I guess it's only fair. He needs to know where I am.

Our progress is slow in the thin air and deep snow. The sun comes up and soon it is surprisingly hot. You wouldn't expect to be hot at 24,000 ft. But the combination of heavy exertion, the lack of any filtering effect of the atmosphere, and the reflecting action of the snow makes for a kind of solar-oven.

"Avalanche!" Steve calls out.

I hear its crack and rumble and I've already looked up before his warning cry.

I can follow its cloudy progress as it cascades down the chute. I don't see Steve but I'm sure he will be able to duck behind a ledge. I tuck myself in as tightly as I can to the face. I feel the cold rush of air and I'm treated to a light pelting of tiny ice crystals as the main body of the avalanche roars past.

"You all right?" I shout up the slope.

"No problem," comes Steve's snow-muffled reply.

These small avalanches are a daily occurrence as the sun loosens the pack. But we're always wary of the big one. On Annapurna I was caught in a slab avalanche in which I could have bought the farm had I not had my wits about me. I remembered to use the American Crawl. You have to try to actually swim with an avalanche—laying out flat—stroking and kicking exactly as you would in water. Using this technique, it's possible to remain on top of the snow and swim along with it. In fact, in my case I was able to not only survive the avalanche but also the fall. I was swept over a one hundred foot cliff with the flowing snow, but the main body of the slide itself acted as a cushion, so that it was almost like body-surfing a big wave and riding it onto the beach. The snow swept me into the cwm and deposited me on the upslope, where I was able to simply step ashore with a few bruises and a broken wrist after riding the thing out.

At about 1:00 PM we arrive at the point we had predetermined as camp four. We set up the two tents, stash the supplies we had carried, including the two extra oxygen tanks, have a quick lunch of peanut butter crackers and hot tea before heading back down as the weather begins to deteriorate.

Steve points down. We see the clouds roiling up from the valley, thousands of feet below us. They look so soft. I always have to resist the urge to jump. The soft gray cloud-tops look as inviting as a feather bed. The weather here comes up from below. Where we are, it is still beautiful, calm and sunny.

Stuck in one of the tents at camp three through a day of foul weather, I take up my book again.

My lecture was scheduled for the library. At a desk

to my right a woman sat behind a pile of my books. An empty chair beside her waits for me to occupy it. I will smile and sign copies of my book. The backdrop to my podium was a bookcase, with books, of course, but also containing small plaster busts: Plato, Shakespeare, Mozart, Beethoven, Joyce.

In the audience I spotted the usual types, women in their 40's, obviously English Department, men: 40's and 50's—lots of corduroy and leather elbow patches. I was pretty sure that most of these twelve or so would rather be somewhere else, but had been more or less ordered by Laskowski to show up.

There were also students. Several of the young men appeared to be near sleep, as they sprawled in their desk chairs. The young women seemed more alert. On the desks before each of them was a blue 5"x7" file card. Unless there had been a big sale of blue file cards, I guessed that these cards had been issued by instructors, to be stamped at the conclusion of the lecture, as proof of their owner's attendance at a cultural event.

After my reading, which was received with polite applause and followed by a few questions, I took my seat at the table and made small talk with a few of the faculty and students who bought the book. I paid special attention to the girl in the audience who had gazed at me with a dreamy expression throughout my reading. She told me that she had read all my books and was, in addition to being an aspiring future author, an avid outdoorswoman.

"Someday I want to come to Montana and Idaho. I'd love to go backpacking there," she said.

"You really should," I said. "And soon— before the Republicans haul it away or burn it down."

She hoped to get out that way this summer although as yet, she apologized, "I've never made it west of the Grotto."

She was tall and healthy looking. She specialized

in the unmade-bed look, despite the pretty face that lurked beneath a ragged pad of short purple hair that seemed to have been chewed to its present length by some animal.

Her name was Amber.

I wrote "To Amber, I look forward to the day that you will sign one of your books for me. Kenton."

I watched her walk away. She turned back after reading the inscription and smiled.

After the signing, I was accompanied by the department chair and a few of the faculty to the student center for lunch in the grill. This I knew, was a polite but hurried final assignment to those members of the department who could spare a few minutes before their next class. At the exit to the library, Amber waited to squeeze my hand one last time. As she did so, I felt a slip of paper transfer from her palm to mine. Our eyes lingered a moment as I discreetly slipped the note into my pocket.

In the bathroom of the student center I took it out with a sense of pleasant expectation and read. "Party tonight, 8:00. 231 West Judson."

*

Outside the tent, the snowy hurricane has attenuated to a light gale. Here and there, a star peaks through the diminishing clouds. Greg pops in to tell me that I'm to be on the initial summit team.

"Steve is suffering from high altitude cough," he says. "He's afraid he's cracked a rib. I'm teaming you up with Chris Davies. We've got at least a twenty-four hour window in the weather and you'll need to be ready to go at four AM. I want you and Chris to head up to five as soon as the wind dies."

Greg shakes hands and heads back out into the dying gale.

"Good luck."

I read for another hour before I start packing up.

I am excited that I will get the chance to summit, but I'm not crazy about being Chris's partner. I trust Steve and, while I have nothing against Chris, I've never climbed with him. With Steve, the synchronous moves necessary on the mountain are as familiar the steps of a regular dance partner. You never know, with a new partner, how he will react in a critical situation. We are all too aware of how things can and often do go wrong in these conditions. Almost every surviving member of the ill-fated'96 Everest expedition had some convincing story as to why he was not responsible for the deaths of his climbing partner.

In the early afternoon, the wind dies down. Chris and I begin the trek up to camp five. The going is slow in the fresh powder, and we have to punch steps with our boots, each leg sinking in to the knee. Leading is the most exhausting, so we take turns. We pass the unoccupied camp four along the way. We each pick up one of the stashed O2 canisters from the tents there to add to the cache at five. After six hours of this punishing climb, we reach the partially buried tents that Steve and I had set up three days before. I have been on oxygen for the entire trip up from four, but Chris is intent on doing the entire mountain without supplemental O's.

We eat a meal of high-energy bars, rice and tea before hitting the bags. We clean up and say our goodnights. We set our watch alarms for 4:30. The idea, as always, is to make the most of the calm morning hours, ascending the final steep 2000 feet to the summit and head back down by 1:00PM. I'm always amazed at how long it takes. Back home I can make the final 2000 feet of a four-teener in about an hour. From this altitude, we will be pushing it to get there in seven. Chris makes radio contact with base to let them know everything is go. I pick up my book again.

When I arrived at 231 West Judson, I found a typi-

cal college rental house on a street filled with similar houses: front porches littered with green 55 gallon trashcans, upholstered furniture with stuffing bubbling from rips, broken porch swings and the like. Twenty years earlier the neighborhood had probably been home to middle class locals and college professors who had since made their escape to the suburbs, becoming slum-lords for the itinerant student populace.

The house was dark and it sure didn't seem like a party.

My footsteps on the wooden porch sounded hollow and lonely. I was feeling a bit depressed at the sight of the faintly recalled squalor of my own student days, as well as the disappointment over my anticipated encounter with Amber, but I knocked anyway. There was no answer.

"Good," I told myself, "you shouldn't be having these thoughts anyway. "You're a happily married man. Nobody home. This is a sign. You'll go on back to the motel and do a little work on the laptop."

I started to turn away when the door opened and I found myself looking into Amber's lovely face. I knew she was young—too young for an old fart like me—but in the soft light of candles flickering in the room behind her, she appeared to be even younger than a typical college student.

"Am I early? I thought there was a party."

"No," she said. "You're cool. You're the only guest."

She smiled, took my hand and led me to the couch. She relieved me of the very "adult" bottle of wine I had brought. What was I thinking? Instead she handed me a beer and a smoldering paper tube that gave off the long forgotten aroma of my grad school days.

We sat for a while on the couch, me like the adult I am, Amber, barefooted, hugging her knees, which she pulled up under an ankle-length diaphanous skirt. She

quizzed me on my book, hiking and outdoorsmanship.
"Have you eaten?" she asked.
"I had a big lunch with the folks in the department.
That was plenty."
"Let me fix you something. I haven't eaten yet."
I watched her expertly stir-fry vegetables in a wok.
She opened the wine I had brought and stirred it in with
the mix. The aroma of cooking wine brought with it a sud-
den pang of guilt. One of Jennifer's special dishes is
chicken abruzzi. After dinner we talked more and listened
to her music, the same music I used to listen to as a stu-
dent: Neil Young, Dylan, Cat Stevens (when he used to be
Cat Stevens.) Later I discovered the pleasures of unusually
pierced body parts and was treated to a sort of tattoo art
appreciation course.

Shortly after the 4:30 wake-up call, and a final
check with base, Chris and I are on our way up the lee-
ward side of the ridge. I go for as long as I can without
supplemental oxygen but it isn't easy. At least we're tem-
porarily out of the deep snow, as scouring winds on this
unshielded face have stripped the rock practically bare.
Chris leads and I can tell he's getting somewhat impatient
with me as I lag further and further behind.

"We've got a hell of a long way to go," he points
out to me when I finally make it to where he has been
waiting.

I understand his impatience. Resting in the cold
while you are waiting for your partner to catch up, knowing that he will have to rest again when he arrives, is no
fun.

"You're going to have to turn on some O's." he
tells me. "You're looking kind of blue."

I nod my head. I really don't have the strength to
waste on words at this point. He reaches behind my pack
and turns the knob and I feel immediate relief and warmth
as oxygenated blood begins to feed my dying cells once

more. I look up to where the snow slope seems to curve downward, but I'm not fooled. That's not the top. When we reach the spot that had been the downsloping horizon, the sight is disheartening. Now we see the true summit. At my current slow rate of ascent, I am an anchor, weighing down a much stronger climber.

"Look, Chris, I'll never make it before our turn-around time. It's almost noon now. It would be 2 or later before I could get there. You've come this far. Go on. I'll be fine. I'm going back down to four and I'll wait for you there."

"But it's less than a thousand feet. Look at your altimeter. We'll rest here a while. Turn up your O's to wide open. When it's gone you can have my canister. I'm fine and I'm not using it anyway. On the way down you won't need as much and we've got two more back at camp."

I can see that he doesn't want to be a bad partner, yet he doesn't want to give up the dream himself.

"All right," I say. "Just give me a few minutes."

We sit behind a boulder, protected from the biting wind, but the ambient –15 degrees is a killer without enough oxygen in your system. I watch the precious minutes tick away until reluctantly, I tell him I'm ready. But after only twenty minutes I'm exhausted again. I look back and see a figure following me. He's dressed in a black overcoat and carries a cane. The man seems to want something from me. Food? Money?

No.

It's my father. He's unhappy with me about something. But it can't be my father. My father has been dead for years.

"No! Go away! I don't have anything for you." I wave the figure away. But he is pointing at me in an accusatory way. I stumble and begin to slide down the slope. I get my wits about me enough to arrest with my ice axe.

Chris is here now. He helps me back to safer ground. I'm still watching the man in black, pointing. Chris follows my gesture with his eyes. He doesn't seem to care that the figure is now approaching.

"Don Giovanni," I mutter.

"What?"

Chris reaches behind me again for the knob. Nothing. The tank must be empty. He removes his own tank and replaces mine with it. I feel life returning to my muscles—and my brain. After I get relief from the tank I look around for the black figure but he's gone. I decide that it is best not to bring up the subject again.

"You go on," I say. "I know you'll make it. Take the tank. I can make it back to the camp. I'll be fine."

But he won't hear of it. He's going on without the oxygen.

We say our goodbyes and agree to maintain walky-talky contact every hour. I feel fine now, almost giddy, as I begin my careful descent to camp five on oxygen. I turn to watch Chris' progress upward but he has already disappeared behind a ridge.

In the hour since Chris and I parted, the weather rapidly deteriorates. The radio in my pack crackles. It's Greg from base.

"Doug, Chris . . . come in."

"Doug here."

"What's going on up there? Over."

I stop my slow downward progress to respond to Greg.

"I'm heading back to five," I tell him. "Anoxia."

It's hard to talk at all, let alone while descending. I have to remind myself to watch each footfall carefully. One slip and I won't stop sliding for 3000 feet.

"You mean you did not make it to the top?"

"Negative, but Chris went on."

"Where is he now? Over."

I can't answer immediately as I have to keep removing and replacing my mask.

"Chris, do you read? Over"

"Yeah, I'm here. I haven't heard from him for a while. I'll call you back when I make contact."

"We can't get anything from here," Greg says. "You'll have to relay info. But you guys have got to get down. The weather is coming in fast. It looks like it's going to get pretty nasty."

"Right. I'll get back to you."

In the few minutes I sit talking with Greg, the wind picks up and it begins to snow. Tiny ice pellets rapidly adhere to the wind-scoured yellow rockband. It is imperative that I get down to the relative safety of the snowfield where we placed the tents. For a moment I consider trying to contact Chris, but I need to move. Besides, he must be aware of the worsening weather conditions. Surely he has summited by now and is on his way down.

At last I am out of the rocks an onto the snowfield. Visibility is down to zero. After ten minutes of wandering around looking for the tents I get down on my hands and knees to carefully probe the snow ahead of me. The snowfield is about thirty feet across and maybe 200 feet long. If I go too far to the left it's a slide into the Western cwm. I know there's a cornice on my right. I punch with my hand. If I break though the cornice with my full weight—I will make a sudden, illegal entry into Tibet.

Wait! I see something. It's . . .it's the man in black again.

It can't be.

I know what this means. I reach back to find the knob but it's already turned as far as it will go. I stand up to face the apparition now approaching.

"Wait," I say. I stumble and begin to slide. I'm resigned. This is it. It's over.

But my slide is arrested by something soft— the

tent.

Once inside, I remove my gloves, crampons and boots. I can't feel any of my fingers or toes. Chances are I will lose a few of them at best. Crawling around in the snow was not a good idea but I had no choice. I breathe from the stashed O2 tank and my mind clears once again. After a few minutes I turn down the flow. If I am going to get out of this I have to conserve as well as keep the other tank full for Chris. When he makes it back he is definitely going to need it and I'm not taking "no" for an answer this time.

I try the radio. "Chris do you read? Come in."

Nothing. I decide to read a bit and try again later.

When I last left the protagonist, Brian, he had spent a sensual evening with his young protégé, Amber. The one-night-stand had left him satisfied and he was now back at home in Montana with his wife and kids, *"feeling a bit guilty over my indiscretion. But Amber was, after all, three or four states away, depending on the route one took."*

Chapter 19

"Would anyone like more wine?" Jennifer asked.

Her mother shook her head and covered the empty glass with her hand. Her father and our guests, Brad and Susan all accepted the offer, as did I. Jennifer's father was in the middle of his often repeated story of the time Jennifer had come home from a camping trip with an injured great horned owl. Jennifer and I were quite familiar with his tale of the family cats who had watched in terror as Jennifer nursed the animal back to health in the garage. Just as he was getting to the day she and her dad drove the owl back to where Jennifer had found it, the phone rang.

"It's for you," Jennifer said as she laid the receiver down and returned to the table.

"Who is it?" I whispered to her, on my way to

answer. She shrugged.

    "Hello."

    "Hi!"

    "Yes? Sorry, to whom am I speaking?"

    "It's me. Amber."

    "Oh . . . yes . . . hello."

I was aware of the laughter coming from the table. I felt myself perspiring and turning red. Jennifer was look-ing my way. If only I were back at the table listening to the boring story again.

    "Excuse me for a second," I said into the phone, covering the mouthpiece with my hand. "It's about a lec-ture they want me to do," I mouthed to my wife. "I'm going to take it upstairs." I pointed to the phone; then pointed up the steps with my finger, as if Jennifer had no idea where exactly, the upstairs of our house was located.

    "I'm here," Amber explained.

    "You're . . . where?"

    "Here, in Bozeman. Remember when you said you'd like to take me camping? Well, this is your chance."

    There was silence from my end.

    "Well?"

    "Look . . .Amber. That was a one-night thing. I told you that I was married. I didn't lie to you."

    "No but I bet you didn't tell your wife everything about your visit to Southwest Iowa. If I were you, I'd arrange a little camping trip. She might take too kindly to all of your workshop activities."

    Just then Jennifer stuck her head around the cor-ner.

    "Are you going to be much longer? Mom and Dad are going soon."

    "Uh . . .yeah just a second. "Excuse me Miss . . ." I said into the phone.

    "Let's say, Snyder," Amber said.

    "Miss Snyder, I'll be with you in just a second."

I put my hand over the phone again. "They want me to come do this signing in Minnesota and it's a rush job. I'm trying to figure out what I can come up with here. I'll be down as soon as I get it worked out."

Jennifer clapped her hands. "Minnesota? That would be great. I'll come with you. I could visit Kathy and Dave in Minneapolis."

"Uh . . .did I say Minnesota? I meant Missouri. I got the M's confused. Anyway, I'll be down in a few minutes."

I saw Jennifer give me a puzzled look before she disappeared around the corner.

"OK, Where are you?"

"I'm staying at the Mountain View. It's a little dump off highway 86. Let's go to Canada. It's not that far and I've never been. Oh, and Brian. . .I've got good news and bad news."

I braced myself.

"The bad news is, I just now got my period. But," she said, *" the good news is that at least you don't have to worry about . . .**that**!"*

"Good." My mind explored some possibilities suggested by this information. This little infidelity was looking like big trouble. "We'll see," I said. I don't think I can go to Canada, but maybe we could go to . . .Glacier."

"Brian!" Jennifer called from the bottom of the stairs.

"Coming! Listen I gotta go. What room are you in?

"114. But I don't have much money. I can't stay here more than another day."

"Don't worry about that. I'll try to see you tomorrow."

The radio crackled. "Doug, do you read?"
"Chris, You OK?"
"It's Greg. Have you heard from him? ..ere ...r

you?"

"Negative. I'm good. I'm in t
probably have frostbite. I can't reall'
"..'ll just have to ..ay there u
We'll send someone for you. Let u;
Chris. Over."

"Roger that."

I try Chris on the radio. Nothing. It's been five
hours now since we separated.

I return to the book.

At last I hear static and a faint voice. "Doug? Base,
Anyone?"

"Chris, where are you?"

"I'm not sure."

His voice sounds weak and tremulous.

"Maybe five-hundred feet below the step. I couldn't see at all so I dug a snow cave. I'm in my bivvy sack. I
don't know man. Don't think I'm gonna make it."

"Hang in there." I say. "Keep moving. Don't sleep.
You know what I'm sayin?"

There is no answer.

I relay the bad news to base. I only know of about
four climbers who have ever survived a bivouac above
27000.

I read into the next chapter, Brian and Amber head
up to Glacier. Amber is happy. She opens a bottle of wine
in the car and breaks out plastic glasses from the motel.
Brian is a bit grumpy about the situation but loosens up
after a few glasses.

*"This will be so much fun," Amber tells me. "I
could move out here and we could see each other a lot.
Who knows what could happen?"*

"Yeah," I said, trying to disguise my lack of enthusiasm for her plan, "who knows?"

They strap on their packs. Brian carries his two-man tent, extra water, and his water purification kit and

Redneck Joyride

.ead off into the woods.

At the trail-head, Amber started to sign the regis-r, but I stopped her.

"You gotta understand. I don't want to check in. I'm supposed to be lecturing in Missouri."

I had called Jennifer from the road in theoretical Colorado. Taking one of my scenic routes, I would be on the road for a few days.

"I'll check in now and then when I can get cell reception," I told her.

Jennifer was aware of the near uselessness of my digital cell service when off the beaten track of the inter-state system. She was used to being out of touch with me for long periods.

We started out on a trail that had a reputation for heavy bear activity.—Amber, I reckoned, must be in the second day of her menstrual cycle. Along the trail toward the divide I pointed out various western wildflowers: long stemmed blue flax, low-growing scarlet globemallow, blue columbine, Wyoming paintbrush . . . I have to catch myself before calling it Indian paintbrush, now a politically incorrect nomenclature. But I do not point out bear-sign that she would not recognize—telltale scratches on trees we pass, and off to the side of the trail—bear scat. We set up camp at the edge of a glacial lake.

I look up from my book and check my watch. I try Chris again. After a few minutes I hear a weak response.

"Doug. I'm not going to make it."

"Are you moving?"

"Trying . . . but . . .can't . . .feel . . ."

His voice trails off and I lose reception. Outside the tent, the wind is still howling and the noise of the rip-pling fabric is deafening. It's hard to make out anything from the radio even when I can make contact.

I relay the situation to Greg at base again.

"Keep us informed," Greg says, "If the weather breaks, we'll send a rescue up from three as soon as they can get going. How are you?"

"Cold, but I'll make it."

After we cooked and ate our freeze-dried meal, Amber offered to clean up but I wouldn't hear of it. I pretended to wash the pans thoroughly down at the lake edge but left the pan with the heaviest food smells and even a few scraps still in it tucked behind a rock about twenty feet from the tent. We sat on our sleeping pads down by the lake and huddled together, wrapped up in one of the unzipped bags. Amber gasped when a shooting star blazed across the horizon. Against the darkness, its temporary blilliance actually caused earthly objects to cast faint shadows. Its passing reflection flickered across the glacial lake.

We fondled a bit under the warmth of the bag, but she reminded me, "You know, I can't do anything for a day or two."

"Right," I said. "I forgot."

The radio comes to life, reminding me again of the reality of my present situation.

"Doug. Do you read? Over"

"Chris? Thought we had lost you man."

"Still here. I've been trying to get through. Somehow I'm feeling better. It's getting lighter up here. I'm going to try to move. I'm going to see if I can make it down to you. Signing off to conserve battery. Over."

"Roger."

I relay to Greg. He tells me to get out of the tent when it's light and watch for Chris.

I attempt to extract myself from the bag but my body objects to the effort. Also my tank is nearly empty. It probably would have held out longer if I had been sleeping and breathing shallower. I get the tank I've been saving for Chris and open it up full. Still I can't bring myself

to go out into the cold. I can tell though, that the weather
is improving. The winds have abated and it's getting
lighter by the minute.

I call base. "Greg?"

"I read ya."

"How's the weather down there?

"It's still bad here. What about you?"

"I went out for a few minutes," I lie. "Can't see a
thing."

"Roger that. Listen Doug, It doesn't look like we
can get a rescue up in time. If it clears, and you can do it,
we need you to try to get to him. Take the extra tank."

"Greg , . . . couldn't . . . ead . . ast . . response." I
hold the radio next to the flapping fabric. "I'm signing off.
. . conserve battery."

*I made sure that Amber had plenty to drink before
we crawled into the tent.*

*"Don't want to get dehydrated at elevation," I tell
her.*

*I laid awake for most of the night . . .listening.
Under my body I have left the "on" button of my little
flashlight pushed in. I heard a faint rustling of brush and
the light clank of metal on rock. Amber was still snoring
gently next to me. At about four she woke.*

"Gotta pee," she said. "Can I borrow your light?"

*"Sure." I fumble around and pull the thing out. I
punch the button but only a feeble glow can be seen from
the tiny bulb.*

"Damn. Must've left it on when I fell asleep."

"Oh well." she says, "The stars are out."

I flip the switch on the radio again.

"Doug, you read?"

I don't answer.

"Doug, come in. I must be somewhere near you
now. Can't see. I'm snow blind. Can you hear
me?—Doug?"

I look out the tent flap. In the distance, I think I see a dark point. I watch it for a while. Doesn't seem to be moving. It must be a rock. I close the flap against the biting cold. I just can't stand the idea of going out there.

I switch the radio off.

I listened as Amber crunched her way over the gravelly terrain down toward the lake. It's so quiet that even from here I could hear her tinkling. Then . . .a gasp. I lean up on my elbow to listen. I hear a series of short, breathy feminine gasps.

"Oh . . . oh. . .Oh God!"

The sounds are almost orgasmic.

Then. . .a scream . . followed by more staccato protestations then another, this time more muffled, gurgling scream.

"Oh god!" "It hurts! He's killing me!"

I noticed that she said, "He's killing me." What does she think is happening I wonder?

"Oh please help me! God . . .it's . . He . . .

Silence.

I listened intently for a few moments without moving. No more sounds came from the direction of the lake. Then I heard the sound of ripping fabric and a crunch. Bones breaking?

It's quiet again. I wait, listening, but Amber does not return.

I switch on the radio. Nothing. I leave it on but hit the mute.

In the morning I packed everything except Amber's bag. I didn't want to check down by the lake but couldn't resist a peek in that direction. I saw something red . . .a scrap of fabric? She had been wearing a red sweatshirt. Just beyond the red scrap, there's something else. I squinted, trying to make the thing out. What is that? It's . . . an arm. At the end of the severed appendage, an accusing finger protrudes from the mangled flesh —pointing at—me.

Her wallet was still in the tent, along with her glasses and some other effects. I pocketed a video rental card with her signature. I put the wallet back in her sleeping bag and left the other stuff with the bag. At the trailhead I did the best I could at forging her signature into the register from the card.

I check the radio again. The battery is dead. When I look out, the weather is clear. The dark spot is still where I last saw it on the ridge. From below I hear distant voices calling: "Chris . . .Doug"?

Just a few more pages to go. But I need to get out of here. I pull myself out into the snow. They'll be here soon. I stumble up the ridge about fifty feet. I can see the dark point a little more clearly now. The voices are closer now. I fall down in the snow face first and drop the dead radio in front of me. I stay put, pretending to be unconscious. When they reach me, Peter Louden revives me with fresh oxygen. I've been off the stuff for about ten minutes now and it sure feels good to be back on it. Pemba and Ang Lhakpa run on toward the dark thing where they drop to the snow. They seem to labor frantically over the spot. At last, the two Sherpas return to see about me.

"We lost him," Peter tells me after a hand-signal-aided discussion with Pemba. "You must have collapsed here. He was only hundred-fifty yards from the tent."

The rescue team does its best to carry me when possible but I have to walk on my own over the steep faces. In my pack I carry the Kenton Borden book. I can finish it at base.

The day after my return, Jennifer and I were reading the morning paper in bed with our coffee.

"Did you hear about that girl up at Glacier?" she said.

"No. What?" I asked, casually turning the pages of

the sports section.

"Killed by a grizzly. Apparently, she was camping alone. They think she may have been menstruating. They always seem to want to blame it on that. They haven't found the bear yet."

"Yeah," I said, "people should know better than to hike in alone. Probably no bear-bells or precautions of any kind. Probably didn't clean up properly after cooking."

"That was kind of strange actually," Jennifer said. "They found one pan that still had scraps of food in it. But there were no utensils, no tent. But here's a really interesting thing. She was a student at that school in Iowa, where you went to lecture."

"Hmm."

"I think I still have the article. Maybe you met her. Maybe she came to your talk."

"Maybe. But you know . . .I didn't take names."

When I get back to the States, I'm hospitalized for a few days. They have to remove the tips of two fingers from my left hand and I lose a toe from each foot, but I consider myself lucky.

Poor Chris.

There was nothing I could do. I tried to go out but conditions were impossible— then the radio died.

I get out of bed to go to the bathroom. In the mirror I see that I'm very thin. Lost about seventeen pounds. I always lose weight on these expeditions. Damn. I look pretty good. I usually put it back on in a few weeks but this time I intend to try to keep it off.

Plasma

5:38. The artist awakes. It's too early to get up, but the dream has come with a set of instructions. He stifles a laugh. The artist's wife rolls over to touch his shoulder.

"Are you all right?" she asks.

"Yes," he says, "I —"

She hushes him with a finger to his lips. He remembers that he should not use his regular voice. The slightest sound will alert the upstairs cat.

"I had the dream," he begins again in a whispered tone.

But it's too late. The upstairs cat is young and possesses acute hearing. They feel the thump as it jumps from its couch. More thumps as it descends the stairs to lie between the bottom step and the door. The upstairs cat waits there—listening.

It begins to yowl.

"In this dream," the artist continues in his regular voice (the damage done), "I am disassembling a machine with numbered parts. The numbering begins at 1,489 and goes back to a single part, labeled part number 1-13."

The artist's wife responds to this information with gentle snoring.

He gets up. He leaves the bedroom with its sleepers, wife and dog, and closes the door. He attends to the morning duties so that he can begin to build part 1-13 through part 1,489. He feeds the upstairs cat, the downstairs cats and the studio cat. The studio cat is actually a stray, brought in on cold or rainy nights. Yet another outdoor cat shows up when he emerges from the house to retrieve the paper. He feeds the animal.

He grinds the coffee quietly, lifting the machine from the counter so that its vibrations will not be amplified through the acoustics of the cabinet. At last he can begin the work for which the dream has made him eager. He makes a drawing of the thing, extracted from memories of the dream—already fading. He must work fast, as the instructions blur and mingle with images of hungry cats and coffee grinders. In his studio he finds materials for parts 1,489 through 1,484. These parts he names, as the dream has instructed, the hammer, anvil, stirrup, bludgeon and dustpan.

The artist and his wife have jobs to support themselves and the dog and cats who live with them. The artist's wife leaves for her job at the bank where she has advanced to the position of head-teller. The artist, who cannot possibly complete the art with its many parts in a day, leaves the collection of completed and yet-to-be-completed parts on his work-table next to the exploded-view plan, assigned to him by the dream.

He rides his Honda motorcycle, manufactured to resemble a Harley Davidson motorcycle, to his workplace.

The university pays him to coax young people to build or make pictures of the art that lives inside their heads. The parents of these young people expect them to make money from their ideas so that they can own homes and drive automobiles like the ones the young people grew up in and rode about in.

"Boy, are they going to be surprised," he says to himself.

After a week of construction, the art is nearly finished. To complete it, the artist needs only to buy from Radio Shack, a small unit, which will house four linked 9-volt batteries. But he cannot do this tonight because the artist's wife has invited some of her co-workers from the bank to dinner. Before dinner it is his responsibility to provide drinks for and chat with Harold Kinsolving, Harold's wife Janice and the Randals, Mitch and Babe. It is difficult for the artist to call Mrs. Randall "Babe" but he knows that he must.

"So," says big Harold Kinsolving to anyone listening, "did you see that game the other night? Shit. I turned it off when the Cats were down 24-17."

"Yeah. When I saw the final score, I thought, what the hell? Is this a basketball game?" says Mitch.

The artist understands that they are speaking of sports. The women talk of recipes.

"It's a banana-chocolate-peanut butter pie," says Babe of her new creation. "I got the idea watching this pie-making contest on the Food Network."

Sometimes the men make an effort to include the

artist in their conversation: "So how are things at the university?" Or, "I hear they've got the inside track on that that quarterback from Adair county."

Harold asks him about his work.

The artist explains that he has been chosen to produce a new piece.

"What?" says Harold. "Like a grant or prize or something?"

"I have been chosen," the artist says.

The artist's wife intervenes, suggesting that the artist give their guests a demonstration of the new 42 inch-plasma television.

He demonstrates the clarity of a DVD displayed on the apparatus.

Harold Kinsolving offers to bring some beer and pretzels over on Sunday to watch the game with him on this device.

The artist has no response to this. He considers saying, "I have no response to this," but thinks better of it and sips at his drink instead.

Harold looks around awkwardly at the art displayed throughout the house but, like the artist, has no response. Each person fidgets with his or her drink or napkin. Babe examines a coaster, as if that is the object of great curiosity rather than the artist. Fortunately for all concerned, the artist's wife suggests that they all come to the table.

When the guests leave, the artist and his wife clean up and he returns to the studio for some tweaking.

"Don't stay up too long," the artist's wife says, and he does not.

In the morning he acquires the necessary parts from Radio Shack (which he calls Radio Shark because that sounds better to him). He must be careful not to write checks made out to Radio Shark or Snake Farm Insurance or Pizza Hat.

He completes assembly of the art and flips the switch, which sends power, surging from the nine-volt batteries, through its innards. The art shudders and a humming can be heard, but beyond that, it does nothing. The artist is not disappointed because he does not know what to expect from the art and is content to wait for further action at an undetermined time. He leaves for work on the Honda motorcycle that resembles a Harley Davidson motorcycle.

In the evening the artist and his wife arrive home at the same time. They greet one another with a kiss and approach the front door. They stop upon hearing noises from inside the house. These are generally the kinds of noises that are unwelcome in ones' home. They are the sounds of breaking glass and crashing metal, noises like that.

The artist cautions his wife to go no further than the front porch with a gesture recognizable the world over, to signify "halt."

He creeps through the rhododendrons to peek into the window. He sees no signs of life in there, in the forms of cats or dog, but after a while he notices a movement. It

is the art, which now ranges throughout the house. The art
scoops up a china cup that it has removed from the pie-
safe. It smashes the cup against its anvil with blows from
the hammer and bludgeon. It certainly seems to show no
interest (as yet) in using its dustpan, as a debris field clearly follows in the art's wake.

The artist motions for his wife to join him at the
window. They watch as the art moves off into what they
call the situation room.

"I hope it doesn't get the 42-inch plasma TV," he
says, just as they hear an enormous crash, followed by the
tinkling of glass.

They laugh, both imagining the release of all that
plasma.

They enter the house when things quiet down. On
the floor of the living room, spots of bright red blood trail
away toward the couch.

"Uh-oh," says the artist's wife.

The upstairs cat emerges from behind the couch. It
sits and looks at them with large questioning eyes then
begins to lick at a wounded paw. The artist's wife opens
the door to the upstairs cat's room and it hurries up to its
bowl of dry food.

In the situation room, the art sits silently, brooding
among shards and plasma. It is not a perpetual motion
machine, as there is no such thing, even though it would
like to be. As if to demonstrate this, the art gives a final
twitch as the energy from its battery pack gives up the
ghost.

The artist and his wife begin to assess the damage to their home. The dog emerges from under the bed. All the animals are accounted for, and except for the wounded paw seem none the worse for wear. As the artist's wife sweeps up the mess, the artist scoops plasma into two empty peanut butter jars.

He places the jars of plasma on his bedside table. Each night before turning out the light he examines them by holding them up to the lamp. They look the same except for the lids, because one was Jif and the other was Peter Pan.

So far—nothing.

But one day he is certain, the plasma will induce a new dream. In the mean time he considers amending the art, adding part #1490 which he calls the "wiskbroom."

The artist reviews in his mind what he perceives to be the failure of this art. Then he remembers. In the original dream, he was *disassembling* the art.

The art waits patiently in the vacancy left by the 42-inch plasma TV, for its power source to be renewed.

The Valet

He's late again. The dinner is nothing special, but still, she had prepared it hoping to share one of the moments she looks forward to each day.

Empty Nest Syndrome. That's what they call it.

When she had moved out of her own parents' home for college—for good really, her mother must have felt the same thing, except there was no name for it then. Everything has a name now—a condition tied to it—even a drug to relieve its itch.

She waits. Watches the news. Avoids starting on the opened wine bottle without him—for a while anyway. One glass, during the first of the back-to-back *Friends* re-runs. Those young faces of the long-running sit-com— it makes you sad. Funny really. It's not that they are young that makes you sad. Not that they are younger than you. Not that they have so much of their lives ahead of them and so much of yours is behind you now. It is this: they look so young in *this* early episode, compared to them-selves.

If she sits here long enough, through the second syndicated re-run—if he's not home by then—she can switch to NBC to catch the new one. She can see in their

faces the changes in her own face, her husband's face.
New lines. New wrinkles. The thickening. The effects of
substance abuse. Weight loss. Weight gain.

That one there with the dark hair. She doesn't
change much. Never more or less interesting. Always the
least interesting. Must be anorexic.

She feels her own waist, arms, wrists. What would
it be like to be that thin? Would she feel like running? Not
for the health benefits or the lowering of cholesterol, or
the endorphins, but just feel like running, as she had when
she was a girl.

Her wine glass is empty now. She does not need a
refill. She's disciplined. She does not have a drinking
problem. Drinking problems and empty nesters are frequently amigos, she knows. But it won't happen to her
like it did to her friend Sharon. She looks around the
house—their new house in their new subdivision. She
wishes they could have afforded one of the houses in the
older part of Heron's Landing, the lush section for which
the development had been named, the section in which
there is still a small body of water upon which a heron
might wish to land. That's Phase I. The treeless, waterless,
bulldozed newness of her section—Phase II, contains three
or four unfinished houses standing in muddy lots alongside the houses like hers, on sodded lawns and with perfect, small ornamental trees in place of the second-growth
forest that had stood there up until three years ago. Still,
it's nice. Everything is spacious and clean. She has the
kind of space now that she really could have used when

Christin and Todd were growing up.

She walks through the house with her refilled wine-glass, flipping on lights to study each room, her footsteps hollow on the glossy maple. She would have preferred a satin finish but Charles had insisted on gloss. Wanted it to look like a basketball court, he said.

And now here he is. He's sorry he's late. He accepts the wine glass she pours for him and kisses her in the cordial way their years together have allowed their kisses to become. "You remember what tommorow is?" She says.

"Friday?"

She looks down at her fork, starts to lift it to her mouth.

"I'm just kidding," he says. "Do you think I'd forget our anniversary?"

"Well," she says, smiling, relieved, "It wouldn't be the first time."

"I have a gift and everything."

She knows the gift will be fine, nothing extravagant. Some kind of jewelry probably. It doesn't matter. It really *is* the thought that counts.

"Listen," she says. "Let's go out tomorrow. I've never been to Charlie Trotter's. I know it's ridiculously expensive, but I just want to go there one time."

"You think I still have time to take out a second mortgage?"

She looks at him with a pleading expression.

"All right, I'll call and drop a name. See if that

pulls enough weight to get us in on short notice."

She brightens. "And I want to stay at the Drake . . . please."

"Um, what about the Palmer House. I like it there."

"Please," she says. "We've never been to the Drake."

She's thrilled with dinner. They try not to balk at the wine list. No bottle is under $100.00. The fixed menu is outrageously priced but she has starved herself all day to stuff herself tonight. Tomorrow she'll begin the low-carb diet. In two months she will be as spindly as the raven-haired *Friends* star.

He blinks and boggles at the check. She tucks the menus, engraved in gold with their names, pretty as her wedding invitations, into her purse. Before he slides the credit card into its special pocket, he shares the total with her so that she too may boggle at it. With the twenty percent tip the meal comes to a neat $500.

"Good evening, Sir." The valet at the Drake addresses her husband. "I hope we haven't traded the Lamborghini," the man says, eyeing their gray minivan with obvious disapproval.

She catches a note of discomfort from her husband who hands the man the key.

At the desk, the clerk is polite. "Good evening, Mr. Bu . . ."

Her husband coughs loudly.

"Simpson," he says.

"Good evening, Mr. . . . Simpson. Yes, I have your reservation here."

The hesitation is so slight it nearly got by her. The man shifts his eyes almost, but not quite imperceptibly her way and back to the register.

In that brief glance, she understands. She sees that he has registered *her* as well. In that glance he has registered the face of the Midwest, the years of childbearing and childrearing servitude.

The elevator ride, with the silent bell-hop, is quiet, tense. Her husband tips the young man. They fool with the TV. She turns down his offer of a drink from the mini-bar. He pours one of the tiny bottles for himself.

In the bathroom, she runs water in the sink, the shower— repeatedly flushes the toilet—to cover the disgorging of her share of the five-hundred dollar anniversary dinner.

While he's sleeping she gets up and leaves quietly. She takes a taxi to the burbs and its empty nest—to pack.

A Mélange

A Mélange first appeared in the author's first collection of
short fiction entitled Mélange

"I wanna go for a ride."

"I'm always up for that," I tell her. "You been on a
bike before?"

"Sure. It's been a long time, but my dad used to
take me."

I let Jessica get on first. When we take off she puts
her arms around me and rests her face against my jean
jacket. After a few miles I can tell she feels safe because
she releases her hug, and the comforting, close contact of
her breasts against my back disappears.

"Where are we going?" I shout back to her, against
the wind.

"Let's go to the Silver Dome up in Sled Lake."

I don't want to appear to be some kind of pansy.
She thinks I'm pretty macho — I think. But damn, Sled
Lake is fifty miles over the pass. This light jacket and that
cute little yellow sweater are going to seem pretty thin,
especially coming back down after dark.

I guess seeing me at a bar somehow excites her.
I'm probably not too exciting in class, standing there droning on about some long-dead painter or sculptor. They
always seem surprised that we have regular lives, listen to
music — drink beer. I've noticed her, of course. She's
cute, blonde . . . good tits. And that low scratchy voice.
It's sort of like that singer who wanted a Mercedes Benz

— her friends all drove Porches — she had to make amends. What was her name? I can't remember stuff like I used to.

What the hell is that? We slow down and stop about twenty feet in front of the accident scene.

"Oh my god," Jessica says.

I don't see any skid marks, just these two animals, a dog, I think and . . . I don't know what the other thing is. It has big hooves. They're still alive. There's nothing else out here on this dessert highway. You might see a car every five or six minutes. You can see forever out here. We stay for a while watching these two injured beasts dance around one another. A car comes toward us. When it finally arrives on the scene, the driver slows to look, first at us, then at the horrible sight, before speeding away. He doesn't want to get involved. Maybe he thinks it could be catching. There's lots of blood and liquid. I don't know what the liquid is, oil maybe or gasoline, but we see no sign of a vehicle. The dog thing rolls over the big-hooved thing and their juices ooze and mingle. We glance back at the sight as we pull away and start up the mountain toward the Silver Dome.

Jessica, sobered now by the wind and the accident says, "Order me a Bellini."

She sees the look I give her and tells me the ingredients.

"Three parts champagne, one part peach schnapps and a dash of grenadine."

The Silver Dome isn't exactly the kind of place where you order Bellinis, but Jessica would like to reestablish the comfortable numbness she left at the Madison Bar and Grill. Just so they don't get any funny ideas, I order a Coors for myself before reciting Jessica's recipe.

"We don't got Grenadine, schnapps or champagne," the bartender tells me. "Ya want me to substitute something else?"

Jessica frowns at the taste of her Bellini made from the ingredients the bartender and I agree on, but after two more she's pretty cuddly again. There's something I've been wondering about for three semesters now. I've been wondering what's under those fuzzy sweaters she wears. Not the front. I can tell what's under the front. But the back of her sweaters hides some secret that I have had neither the nerve nor the occasion to ask her about. There is some deformity . . . angular, bony, . . . protruding strangely from the left middle of her back. If she turns a certain way it's gone. Did I really see something? Then she turns again and there it is humping under her sweater like a cat under the bed sheets.

The thing is, I might well be in a position to discover the secret tonight but it sort of scares me. What if I'm repulsed by the mysterious entity living on this pretty young girl's back? What if I'm so disgusted by that great tumor that I can't . . . you know? I could do anything, tumor or no tumor if I had my little blue pills with me. You just need one. I don't know what would happen if I took two of the little suckers although there are plenty of jokes floating around that deal with the consequences of such actions.

The truth is, ever since I heard about the existence of these pills, I have had trouble with the big guy in my pants. The discovery of a pill to remedy a problem of that nature, seems to have made me suddenly aware that there could be such a problem. That knowledge has lived with me ever since, and becomes the center of all thought at just the wrong moments — a self-fulfilling prophecy. When that commercial comes on with the old senator or the one with the well-known athlete who shares my problem I turn it off.

"I can't stop thinking about those poor animals," she says. "What do you think happened?"

"I don't know. Maybe they fell off a truck when it hit a bump."

"What do you think that one thing was?" she says. "It had big feet and hooves but he rest of it was just— I don't know— meat. And I think they were both still alive."

"I don't have a clue," I said. "I want to thank you though, for bringing it up,"

Jessica was leaning heavily into me now at the barstool.

Between the mystery looming under Jessica's sweater and the horrible reality of the bloody fauna on the highway, all hope for success in the arena of amour is rapidly disappearing.

"Let's go back and see what happened to them. Maybe there's still something we can do," she says.

"Like what? I say. "You want me to throw one of them across the passenger saddle and ride into town while you wait there in the dessert in your pretty sweater?"

"No, but let's go see. I just need to find out what happened to them."

I pay the bar bill and we walk out to the bike with our arms entwined.

It's dark now and cold. I look wistfully in the direction of the Antlers Motel next to the liquor store, but we ride on past its red vacancy sign toward the pass.

"I'm so cold," she says. Jessica hugs tightly against my back. My back and her front are the warmest places for miles. If you've never been motorcycle cold, you've never been cold. I remember one night riding home from the town I lived in right after college. It was about two hundred miles to my mom's house. It was her birthday. When I left it had been sunny and maybe sixty-five degrees, but when the sun went down it cooled to about fifty.

At seventy miles per hour, that fifty becomes twen-

ty. I pulled in at every truck stop to hunker over coffee
until my bones warmed up again. The other people in the
restaurant stared at me. It was warm in there but I
remained bundled in my leather jacket and gloves, shivering over my coffee cup.

It takes us twenty minutes to reach the scene. At
first we don't see it. Maybe a road crew has come along
and removed the mess. The unidentifiable animals must
surely have gone to their reward by this time. But no, off
the road about twenty feet now I see it. We ride over and
dismount near the pulsating mass that has dragged itself
away from the highway. I leave the lights on. The head-
light illuminates the thing. On the ground a dark liquid
trail leads from where we had seen the two creatures earlier to what now was a larger singularity. In front of the disgusting mass, two hunting knives lay in the dirt alongside
a shoe.

"I'm-m-m-m s-s-s-oo c-c-cold," Jessica says

Jessica and I both shudder with tremors so violent
that our stomachs knot up.

"L-l-listen," I say.

Off in the distance we hear a barely audible ding-
ing. I walk in the direction of the sound to where I find an
older model Chevy with its driver's door standing open.
The keys are still in the ignition. We could get warm in
this vehicle but when I turn the ignition my only reward is
the clicking sound of a weak battery.

I walk back to Jessica just in time to see her reach
down into the glistening mélange.

"Don't!"

"I'm so f-f-fucking c-c-old," she says as she does a
sort of slow dive into the viscous lump. I hear her give out
a little groan of pleasure as her body mingles with this
bloody potpourri. Jessica's yellow sweater fades to reddish
brown and disappears along with the rest of her.

I'm cold too. Freezing. Oh what the hell. I'm reluctant at first but the thing is so warm. In the cold clear night, steam rises from the mass. I can feel the heat coming off of it. I kneel and stick my hand in. God, that feels good. I push my chest in, then my face. I feel some stirring "down below." I don't think I will need one of those little blue pills tonight.

Doctor's Excuse

"And the motorcycle guy, you never saw him again?"

She looked down at her fidgety fingers.

"I . . .I don't know what happened to him."

"Well that's quite a story," I said, "and I've heard a few good ones. Tell me again about this . . . *glob*."

"Well," Jessica said, "it's pretty disgusting, Dr. Stevens, but I was so cold. The only thing I could think of was getting warm. I'd have done anything. So I went in."

"So, let me get this straight. You see this nasty glob, this unidentifiable lump of flesh on the side of the road."

"That's right," she said, hanging her head.

"And you touch this bloody mess. You get down on your knees and crawl right into this thing. Didn't that make you sick?"

"No. Actually it just felt so good, so — comforting. It was like — like going back into the womb or something. It was so warm."

Her story reminded me of a film I once saw. The leader of a failed arctic expedition had been rescued and flown back to civilization and a hot bath. But he had neglected to tell his rescuers about the location of other members of his party until he was thoroughly warmed . . . and they were thoroughly dead.

"And then . . .?" I asked.

"Well, it was dark at first— warm, wet. But then I saw a light and I was able to sort of . . . swim toward it. Then I was in a room and someone handed me a drink."

"What kind of drink?"

"A Bellini, three parts champagne, one part peach schnapps with a dash of grenadine. I guess they were expecting me."

"Who?"

"The Kennedys, the President, John Junior . . . Bobby. It was a party, very posh and I felt, you know — underdressed. But they didn't seem to mind."

"What about Ethyl and Jackie?"

"Did *they* mind?" she asked.

"No, I mean were they at the party?"

"Oh yeah. They didn't care for me though. They were all like, jealous. The men were pretty friendly to me but the women, well, you know — they're kinda old now."

"But you gotta admit," I said, "except for Ethyl, they're all — you know — kinda dead now."

"Anyway, the party was nice, then I was like 'with' John-John and some of his friends and we went bowling and stuff. And I don't remember much after that. They told me in the hospital that some truck driver found me. I can bring you a doctor's excuse."

"But Jessica, you've missed three weeks of class.

How long did you say you were you caught up in this . . . mélange?"

"I don't know. Time was like . . . *different* in there. I'll make up the work. I'll do — you know — anything."

"I'm sorry. It's still a D. I'm afraid you'll have to go through the appeals process."

Countdown

Cecil Pounders took a peek at his Timex again. 3:27.

He scanned the room, trying to commit to memory its every nook and imperfection. In this snapshot he would keep an account of the hours, the days, the years, the decades of his life that had passed in this room. The photo had changed slightly over time but if he could project this image to anyone else who might be familiar with its circumstances, they could only guess at the era: a hairstyle here, a cuff or gymshoe there.

Across the room the naked young girl was still where he had placed her one hour and ten minutes earlier, on the little bed he had constructed from four rusted car wheels supporting a 4'x 8' piece of plywood — not the good stuff — not the kind they call A/C plywood. Her platform was of the crudest construction-grade sheathing. On this he had placed a piece of foam rubber, covered with a white, or at least what had at one time been a white sheet. Sometimes he felt bad about using the same sheet over and over. It certainly could have used a good washing. He couldn't imagine lying down on such a filthy piece of fabric without cringing.

He had placed her arms around the pillow in a position that he himself found comfortable at night, one arm under, one over, head turned to the side. He liked the pose and sometimes over the years imagined how good it would feel to trade places, with this one or another similar one, and simply go to sleep. She was on her stomach. A beautiful incandescent light played across her shoulder blades, one of which rose in an almost unbelievable angle because of the position of her arms. It cast a shadow as dark as a moon crater across her back in this dimly illuminated room.

Her upper body was parallel to the surface on which she lay while her hips were turned suggestively toward him. As recently as ten years ago he had been somewhat modest about placing them so that their legs were spread apart like this. The lower leg was folded forward, just the foot showing as it doubled back under this side of the straighter upper leg. He had tried leaving their legs together out of his own sense of modesty, but it just wasn't interesting.

Sometimes he forgot the tape, but not today.

This one was blonde, thin but muscular, the way he liked them. The one last week had been pretty — in her clothes — nothing to write home about with them off. Like so many, she had been rather formless, a voluptuous but structureless mélange. The skinny ones had the best bones, cast the best shadows. He thought of Stephanie from — what was it, ten, twelve years back? The sharpened pinnacles of her pelvis had practically erupted from her torso, casting dark shadows similar to that cast by the scapula he now admired.

3:37. Thirty-eight more minutes to go. He had pulled it off. For all these years he had employed this room, its stains, its smells, its parade of changing faces that never aged, as the source of funding for his real work. There would be a dinner, speeches, a gold watch, or at least a special pen, which he would put down on some cluttered shelf, to rediscover from time to time, resurrecting for the briefest moment, this snapshot of his days.

"Are you OK?" he asked the naked girl, expecting no response.

She was asleep.

He always told them that if they needed to get up and move around, they should free to do so.

"Please just try to get back into the same position."

The tape on the sheet marked the bend in the knee, the elbows and the feet. It should help as long as she didn't get confused and reference earlier, ancient pieces of tape. He should have pulled the old ones up but he never thought of it. Besides, you could usually tell, because masking tape hardens into a sort of brittle, yellowed newspaper-like substance over time.

When he placed the tape, he came so close to contacting the naked flesh that he could feel heat. Sometimes, (accidentally?) he actually brushed against skin and often noticed that it responded with goosebumps.

Each of the eight people in the room, except the girl, had something in common. They or their parents had paid for them to be there and — they were all bored. In order to alleviate his own boredom, Cecil often told them stories. He had been telling many of the same stories to his captive audiences for years: stories about sports figures and their performances, many of which had taken place before some of them were born, or stories about his personal exploits, movies he admired, books he had read, artwork that upon seeing for the first time, had made him cry. He read books to them while they worked. He forced them to listen to classical music and opera. But that was no longer as easy as it had once been.

Usually, no one else talked during these solo performances. No one laughed at the parts he felt sure were so funny. His best friend had purportedly stood in front of the same room for an entire semester, holding a plastic duck under his arm. According to his friend's possibly apocryphal account of that term, two years before he and Cecil met, not a single student enquired about the aquatic bird.

Often, the only conversational exchanges were between Cecil and the naked girl, on those occasions when she was awake. The models as a rule were comparatively well versed in the subjects upon which, Cecil expounded. They had often read more than the art majors and were obviously uninhibited. Even though they were decades younger, they seemed to have come from his generation. When clothed, they wore long dresses—lots of beads and dangly things—sandals; neo-hippies living in a time when the real hippies had long since given up their own ideals for the Wall Street of their parents' dreams.

But he was tired. Too tired today to tell stories. Today he was in countdown mode.

Even if he had wanted to, no one would have heard him. The model was sleeping, and each of the students, rubbed or scraped, added to or subtracted from the little rectangle in front of them to the accompaniment of throbbing noises piped directly into their heads from tiny personal electronic devices.

Today was Cecil's birthday. He thought back to other birthdays spent in this same room, birthdays during Vietnam, during the Falklands war, during Gulf I, and now Iraq. He, unlike many of his fellows, welcomed his birthday, because that day always came so close to the end of the school year, meaning he would be out of this room for three months. But back during the Vietnam and Falklands days, he had to spend his summers in this room as well. Otherwise, there would be no money during July and August. Even so, the summer pay was a reduced amount, and the hours spent in the room in September and October—sometimes even part of November, had to go toward repaying expenses incurred during the hot, poorly funded months.

He wasn't supposed to away for long periods of time, leaving a room full of people he didn't know all that well with a naked girl, but he often was. It was too boring.

Of course there were moments when his services were required to help correct a misdirected line here or suggest the reduction of a head drawn five times its actual size there. But most of the time he stood around, watching the clock; watching another segment of his life ebb away.

Some days, after he felt that he had hung around for a respectable amount of time, he would go down the hall to his office. In the old days before computers, he might use this escape-time to read, or to arrange a racquet-ball game with some buddies from accounting. These days, he got on the internet and bought shit on EBAY. Man, you could really lose track of time that way. Sometimes he would head back down to his classroom to find his students packing it in for the day, crossing paths with the model as she padded down the hall in her bare feet and terrycloth robe, already heading for the dressing room.

On those occasions he pretended that he had been called to an impromptu meeting with colleagues, or had been with an advisee when time got away from him. He signed the model's slip when she brought it back into the room, so she could get her ten bucks an hour for sleeping.

*

"You mean there's a naked girl in the room with you?" Russ asked one day in the locker room.

"What if I just sat in? I can't draw a straight line but I'd be real quiet."

"Well," Cecil told him, "She doesn't have any straight lines so you'd probably do just fine. But you'd get bored just like everybody else. I'd let you audit, but you'd have to agree to come every day."

Cecil could see Russ thinking the offer over.

"Is it the same girl every day?"

"Yeah, unless she's unreliable about showing up and I have to fire her."

"Well, no thanks then. I already got the same one

at home every damned day."

*

Ten, nine, eight, seven, ...
"Well, that's it for today. Remember, I'll need to
see your final portfolios next Wednesday at 1:00."
He'd managed to push through another year, and a
whole day in the room without attempting any kind of
escape.
It was over. Yet, something had been nagging at
him over the past few weeks. What if his job was his iden-
tity? What then? Would he become like Ted Jensen? It
seemed that one moment Ted was in the studio around the
corner from his, showing them how to make impressions
from slabs of quarried limestone, or ramming thick pig-
ments through gauzy films to become multiple originals,
and the next time he saw him, he was a tottering old coot,
wanting to know if Cecil had seen the latest episode of
Survivor or Crimestoppers or was it Crimebusters, or
some other crap he couldn't imagine wasting five minutes
on. Is this what happens to you when you finally have
time on your hands?
For thirty years he had nursed every second in his
studio at home until he absolutely had to leave in order to
be in his classroom on time. The clock in his studio,
leaned on a shelf filled with screws and nails and wire and
what-have-you. It was partially obscured by a loop of
woven sticks, part of a project he had abandoned years ago
but didn't want to throw out. He kept his eye on the
minute hand until it reached the forty-minute mark. That
left him five to wash up, five to get a cup of to-go coffee
from the gas station, ten to drive to the building, six to
find a parking space, five for the elevator and he would be
in the room only five minutes late. What now? Too much
time? Would he become Ted?
When he got to his office he found a note taped to

his doorknob. Everyone knew that if the note was attached to any other surface on, or around his door, it would be lost in the myriad of unheeded notes already in place, some as yellowed and brittle as the masking tape on the model's sheet.

Pearson wanted to see him before he left for the day. Probably wanted to tell him about plans for his retirement dinner. The secretary was gone for the day so the outer office was locked. Reluctantly he tapped on the glass. Nothing. But he knew Pearson was in there, avoiding going home until after 6:00, even though the offices on campus all closed at 4:30. What was so bad at home? He could only imagine. He himself had once been married.

"Stan?" he called out at last.

He heard a muffled clank from the inner office, as if he were hoisting the chain of a heavy anchor. What the heck did he do in there? Through the milky diffusion the frosted glass allowed, he perceived the opening of the inner office door and watched as a dark shadow pierced a nimbus of light, floating through the outer office to the door.

"Hey, Cecil, come in."

He stepped into the office but was not welcomed into the inner sanctum, as Pearson blocked his way past the secretary's desk. As he stood awkwardly in the outer office, Cecil felt like Willie Loman.

"You wanted to see me?"

"I did? Oh Yeah . . . hey, I really hate to ask you this but . . . it turns out that the new guy — you know — Shapiro — from New York, well he's kind of eager to get established. He's already rented studio space and an apartment. So, if you don't mind, and I know it's not a really good time for this with finals next week . . . but could you clear out of your office by next weekend? Shapiro'd like to get his stuff in and get started right away."

There was an awkward silence.

"That's his new computer and scanner," Pearson gave a nod to his left, indicating a pile of boxes in the corner. "And I'd really like to get it out of here."

"Ok . . . what do you want me to do with *my* computer?"

"Well, that's such old . . . you know . . . outdated stuff, we'll just send it to . . .you know . . . surplus."

Surplus property. That was what Sherry Edwards the designer, called "the landfill."

"Listen, if you need any boxes, there are plenty down on the loading dock."

Cecil didn't say anything.

"Is there something else," the department chair asked.

"Uh . . .no" He turned to walk away.

"Oh," Pearson said, "I almost forgot. Happy birthday."

*

A few hours slipped by in his office without his really noticing. Despite the mess, it really didn't take that long to box up thirty years of detritus, if one went by Sherry Edwards' rule of clutter disposal: "If you haven't used it in a year, you don't need it."

This was easy. Why had he avoided cleaning this rat hole out for so long? The boxes of stuff he would keep were piled into every nook. Outside the door stood an army of trash-cans that he had appropriated from various studios throughout the building. They bubbled over with papers, folders, files of student-advisees long gone — some in fact — long dead.

Rebecca Alverez. He leafed through the ancient folder. He remembered when Rebecca and two of her friends, all students from back in the first years, had returned to visit him and relive their glory days. That was what—fifteen years ago? He remembered saying to

What's-His-Name as Rebecca disappeared down the hall
with What's-Her-Name to reminisce over their student
days, "Is Rebecca OK? She doesn't look good."

"Ovarian cancer."

She died shortly after.

Then there was AIDS. That took a few of them,
along with the occasional car wreck.

He put Rebecca's file in the "keep" box along with
a dirty, fabric-wrapped mannequin leg that he lifted from
the "still-life storage room." Rebecca's senior thesis show
had consisted of a dark room full of odd sounds accompanied by strange floating figures. Filmy blue fabric made
form-fitting bandages around each plastic torso and
appendage. She had painstakingly pinned the fabric in
place, with thousands, maybe tens of thousands of individual straight pins. Most of the figures had come from the
collection of skeletons and mannequins that had at one
time been clean and whose parts had fit together in anal-
retentive order. Of course, that was before Ron retired.
Nothing Ron touched was ever out of order. But these
days the still-life material was in a mess, scattered
throughout different studios all over the building. And the
one mannequin that Rebecca had left intentionally
wrapped as a remembrance had been used and reused
thousands of times in set-ups with live models, or other
still-life materials. Cecil was the only one left who would
remember her, or how the odd wrapped arm or leg had
come to be that way. The memorial that he felt this item to
be each time he passed over it in favor of a different arm
or leg, had been desecrated a thousand times over. Now he
would take it home with him, maybe have a ceremony and
burial, maybe a ritual Viking-style burning.

It was dark when he left the building and walked
down the hill toward his car. Suitcase U. That's what it
had always been. The town was practically deserted now
at the end of the week before finals. He had seen many

students already stuffing belongings into their cars for the summer. Their profs had probably given finals early, defying the well known edict, so they could get out of town faster themselves. Just as he was about to pull his keys from his hip pocket, a car screeched around the corner and approached, fishtailing at very high speed. He froze and stood innocently watching, as a body popped up through the sun-roof and launched something. He watched, zombielike as the missile's trajectory homed in on him. A perfect strike. An exquisitely planned attack. *Shock and Awe.*

The brown paper bag hit him right in the center of his chest as he, a drone target, stood with books in one arm and his briefcase in the other.

He heard the guffaws and cackles from the car's three youthful occupants as it sped up the hill and disappeared around the corner. Egg ran down his shirt, and rolled over his belt buckle and on down his trousers. He turned and walked back to the building to wash it off as best he could.

He should have been furious, but instead found himself feeling rather numb. He needed a drink. The front of his clothing was wet but he had managed to get the egg and bits of shell off. He strolled into Olivetti's, the only decent restaurant in town that wasn't a chain, all the while glancing from side to side to see if anyone noticed his soaked front. Olivetti's was the only local eatery where you could be assured that five waiters wouldn't descend upon the neighboring table to chant some franchise-mandated butchering of Happy Birthday.

He sat down at the bar and ordered a gin and tonic, which he promptly downed and ordered another. "Make it a double."

It was a few doubles later before he noticed the group of girls at the end of the bar. They were giggling and he saw, tossing looks his way. He took another stiff drink and walked over to them.

"How you ladies doin' this fine Friday evening?"
The two whose faces he could see, took on a frightened-animal look. The girl whose back was to him spun to face him.

"Why don't you fuck off geezer?"
They were both embarrassed at the same moment, as he recognized her as Alicia from his Art 204 and she, with a bit more difficulty, recognized her professor. But the damage was done, and each of them turned pretending they were strangers.

He returned to his station at the bar, but his unfinished drink had been swept away. He ordered another. As he sipped his drink, he caught a glimpse of the recent retiree's reflection between the jewel-like bottles glowing behind the barmaid. He willed the muscles that controlled the optics inside his head, to bring into focus the white stubbly sproutings of his chin and jaw. The large wet spot on his shirt that he had dabbed with wet paper towels in the first floor bathroom of his building, had dried into an unsightly stain of yellow egg residue.

From the pleasant room in the rear of the restaurant, usually reserved for special parties, he heard the muffled sounds of speeches and laughter. Someone's retirement dinner do doubt. It was that time of year. He ordered another drink but the owner intervened without a word by simply resting his hand on Cecil's wrist and with a quiet look that seemed to penetrate his soul, convinced Cecil to settle up and head out.

It was actually good to be outside. The air was cool and the twinkling universe came back into focus. But just as he was about to step into his car, a vehicle came careening around the corner, its three occupants whooping and bellowing louder than the noise made by their conveyance. It sped egglessly passed, but he knew it was *them*. Out of his gin-haze he suddenly remembered the gun that he kept under the front seat. He would find them and teach them some kind of fiery lesson. Even in his current state he was aware of a sort of *punishment befitting the crime* scenario and intended to do something that would be only slightly more injurious to the trio than was his own humiliation, but certainly not fatal. Maybe he would shoot the tires out. Of course he had never been very accurate with the damned thing.

He waited in his car for their next pass through the bar area. When they came he followed. They went left. He went left. He lost them. Three blocks later, and accelerating, he had to make a decision: right or left.

Right. A hard right, which he underestimated by about five inches. He felt the two jolting thumps and heard the sickening cablump, cablump, cablump, cablump of his two passenger-side tires that he had sheared off against the curb.

He was overtaken by a most unpleasant sense of sobriety. The campus cops were notorious for lying in wait for poor drunken students as they *walked* back to the dorms, swaying even slightly. And though he felt sober, he was sure the Breathalyzer would not concur. He could never make it home. He turned the headlights off and continued his mechanized limp up the hill, then down Summit Street. He could hear the metal rims grinding to a halt on the curb in front of the art building.

He let himself in and took the elevator to his office on the fourth floor. But when he opened the door, all the boxes taking up every inch of space jarred his memory. He walked down the hall to the drawing studio, the room that he had not expected to visit again, at least not so soon. He shut and locked the door behind him and lay down on the filthy sheet and slept, dreaming of revenge.

Self Preservation

I awake to what sounds like crackling ice.
In these latitudes? Ice?
Then the all-too-familiar sight greets my con-
sciousness.
I can't recall her face, her voice. I only remember

her body.

I suppose I should have made more of an effort, but . . . at least this way, one of us has a chance. It's not like I really knew her that well . . . and . . . if I ever get back, Janice will never have to know.

Caught two medium-sized dorados yesterday. Almost lost my knife. Not much water left.

I did try—really.

She was snagged in the rigging. I'd have been dragged down with her. It's like those airline safety manuals say: "put the mask on yourself before your child."

She was an island girl. Probably never be missed—in the real world.

Maybe she wasn't even real. People can get delusional.

That must be it. I only imagined her.

It's so fucking hot.

Have I ever been cold? Really cold, like the little Japanese woman on that Everest expedition? How would that feel? Her staring eyes preserved under a sheath of ice. Would I really trade places? If I ever get off this raft, I'll never hold my collar closed against the wind again.

I'll never ask for a table away from the door.

That crackling noise again.

What hit us? Maybe a waterlogged cargo container. Sometimes they wash over the sides of big freighters. A killer whale might have mistaken us for prey. I remember something hitting the hull . . . water . . . swimming inside the cabin, grabbing everything I could. You never know what'll come in handy.

Thank God for the Swiss Army.

My new spear—my knife, lashed to an oar with shoelaces—improves my chances at fishing.

. . . last of peanut butter yesterday . . .

Haven't found a use for the compressed air tank, but I hate to throw it overboard. Tet-ra-fluor-o-ethane—the component stenciled on its side. Nothing else to read.

Recited it over and over, pronouncing each syllable. A mantra.

Fins. Two . . . three.

They've been circling for days.

One comes in close. I strike out with the oar-spear. My knife! Shit. Its red translucence merges forever with the depths. Here he comes again. Grab the air tank, a bludgeon, but it sticks to the bottom of the raft.

Ice!

The valve's slow leak has frozen the wet floor under the canister. When I pull it away, a big chunk of the polyethylene floor rips away with it, replaced by the blue-green sea pouring through.

Smoke—a mast on the horizon.

Too late for that now. I'm going down.

I awake again to that familiar crackling sound.

I open my eyes. Above me, wire-mesh warps the mattress of an upper bunk. I turn to see a bobbing porthole. A Japanese looking sailor sets a glass of water on the table next to my berth. In the glass, the ice crackles again.

the Plug

"Do you think he understands anything we're saying?"

"I don't know honey. He hasn't moved in the whole time I've been here . . .three days now."

"Daddy? Can you hear me? It's Jesse. I brought Robbie . . . isn't he getting big? Go on honey. Say hi to your Grandpa."

"I'm scared."

"Go on. It's OK."

"H . . . h . . . Hi Grandpa."

" Mom, How long's he been facing out that window?

"Well, when I got here this morning they had him facing that way. Sometimes I worry about his eyes — looking out into that light. You know, he never left the house without sunglasses, even on dim days. Maybe we should get some . . . to put on him, you know . . .the light might really be bothering him and he can't say anything."

"How did it happen?"

"Well, you know, he was never sick a day in his life, except for all the knee surgeries and stitches and broken bones and bruises."

"Yeah, I guess he never did quit that damned basketball did he?"

"He got up to go to the bathroom and I heard a noise. You know how soundly I've always slept. But it was loud enough that it woke me and I called out to him to see if he was all right, but there was no answer. When I got to the bathroom he was crumpled by the toilet and there was — some blood. I guess when he went down he

must have hit his head. See. They've put a bandage on his
forehead there."

"Robbie, put that down. — What's that machine
he's hooked to?"

"Well honey, those monitors show heart rate and
temperature, maybe blood pressure, I'm not sure. But that
one is oxygen and I think one of them is food or something that provides nourishment. And you know, there's a
catheter and I guess a bag that does the bowel stuff.
Basically . . .he's . . ."

I know mom. It's OK. You know Tom and I will
always be there for you . . . whatever happens."

"I know, Hon."

"When is Christian getting in?"

"Well, you know Christian — he's always pretty
busy. He's in New York in some important meeting that he
says he's just got to wrap up before he can get away. But
he says as soon as that's done, he'll be on the first flight
out."

"What? That little shit! His bullshit job is . . ."

"Now, Jess, You know Daddy is exactly the same
way. He wouldn't expect anything else."

"I know but, Jesus! For once couldn't he stop
being the big man on campus? So fucking selfish?"

"Shh! Robbie's going to grow up with your foul
mouth. Besides, we don't know. Maybe he does understand what we're saying. Oh dear, he's drooling again.
Here Sweety. Let's get that off you. There. He seems to
drool if I say something that might be meaningful, you
know, other than just small talk. And just then, when you
got upset, it almost seemed like he was responding . . .
you know . . . by drooling. Maybe he does understand."

*Damn right I understand! I just can't do a damned
thing to show it! I wish they'd move the damned bed back
where it belongs. The light is killing me. Let me have a
view of the sink. Fuck. I never thought this would happen*

to me. I did all the right things. Played all that ball for all those years. I always thought that would save me. I'm in great shape. In-fuckin-vincible. Sure, I had all those knee surgeries but the heart and circulation were great. What the fuck happened? This is embarrassing. I must look like a fuckin' moron. This isn't me. I'm a big strong guy. Come on Janie, Jessie, unplug that fuckin' thing!

Do I sleep? I always thought people in this condition were comatose or brain-dead. But I guess they could tell about that, with all that equipment they've got me hooked up to. I envy those brain-dead suckers. Wait a minute. Something's different. This isn't my regular nurse. The view doesn't look the same. Maybe I died. If this is the afterlife, I didn't expect all these monitors and this beeping. Who's this big black dude? He's putting a rubber ball in my left hand. Now he's squeezing my hand back and forth on the ball. That's an odd way for this big guy to get his exercise.

"Hey man, how ya doin today? I'm Clarence. We are going to try to get you back on your feet. I want you to start by trying to squeeze this little ball for me OK?"

No dude. Go away. But pull that plug first. I ain't cooperating. I don't want to come back. I've been through all that rehabilitation shit before. Not this time. Not from something like this. I gotta do more than squeeze rubber to feel like a man. If I got back I would have to be all the way back. Know what I'm sayin' Clarence? I'm just not willing to work that hard any more. I want to be a quitter this time. Hell even Hemingway was a quitter. No offense intended man, but just pull the damn plug.

"OK man. That'll do for today. We gonna get you back."

*Oh shit. Not again. She's always slip'n in here so
they can get it on right in front of me. Like I don't even
exist. Well, I guess they've got a point. Oh good. She's
turned the lights out. There they go. Goin at it like rabbits.
Hey wait a minute. He's bangin that chick up against the
wall where the thing is plugged in. Yeah that's right.
Knock that sucker outta there.*

"Oh Baby . . .Oh Clarence . . .Oh yes . . ."
*Oh yeah. Come on Clarence. Knock that thing
loose. Yes Clarence yes.*
"Oh yeah, Oh, Oh, Ooh . . ."
Yes. They did it. Yes Clarence. Good. They're
leaving quietly. Sneaking out into the lighted hallway.
Good they're gone. I'm feeling so sleepy. Finally, I think
I'm going to get some rest.

Ebay

My executive assistant, Linda looked down at me from the lofty perch of her five-inch heels. The Diet Coke she had placed next to my face, tickled my forehead with it's carbonation. The ice in the glass popped again, completing my state of alertness.

"Oh," I said, trying to appear as dignified as possible, lifting my head from my Madison County Emergency Preparedness Desk Calendar, "thank you, Linda."

I wiped the drool from the side of my cheek and tried to inconspicuously blot its excess runoff from the calendar with my sleeve.

"I'll be leaving for the day then, Sir," she told me. "Will you be needing anything else?"

Each day at 4:30 she brought me a Diet Coke with ice. I would never ask her to, she just did.

When I first awoke, I didn't even remember where I was. I think I had been doing something rather important when I just needed to put my head down for a bit. The door between the inner and outer office is usually open and she hears me shifting papers and so on, but she wouldn't think it was unusual if she heard no sounds for a few minutes. But the last I recall, it was about 3:00. She must have looked in here at least once during all that time. Surely there were phone calls. Someone always wants something from me.

Sometimes I wish I had my old job back. It was easier down in Student Affairs. Of course there were the occasional grumbles about unfairness by some faculty member or a misunderstanding by the parking board, or an injustice at a disciplinary hearing. But I was sometimes the benevolent administrator in those cases, overturning a towing charge here, allowing a Frat-boy back onto the intramural team there. But as president, I have to deal with people's livelihoods or impose upon what they see as *academic freedom*.

"No thanks, Linda. Have a nice evening," I said with a little laugh and a dismissive wave, "I'll see you in the morning."

I shifted a few papers, pretending to be engrossed in the important business on my computer screen, hoping she would leave and I could put this behind me. What *was* it on the screen anyway? As she continued to stand there, my eyes made a quick survey of the little thumbnail images. Then I remembered. I had been looking at—motorcycles— EBAY—before—before what? Someone had been talking to me.

At last there was no recourse but to look up at her since it seemed evident that she was not going anywhere. When our eyes met, hers shifted—twice—toward the far corner of the office where Professor Conrad from History sat in one of the two cozy chairs I kept for visitors. With him was the beautiful young PHD from Cornell that he intended to hire for the vacancy left by the retirement of Randall Clermont. I had the distinct feeling that they may have been there for a while.

At last, Linda turned and left the office. From the outer office I heard the familiar sounds of her packing up for the day, and the clack, clack of her heels to the door and down the hall.

"Yes," I said, "Ms . . . "

"Hernandez," Conrad, reminded me with a little laugh.

"Ms Hernandez, you were telling me about . . ." I struggled to remember where we had left off,— "your research into the utilitarian pottery of the Amazonian Indians of Ecuador."

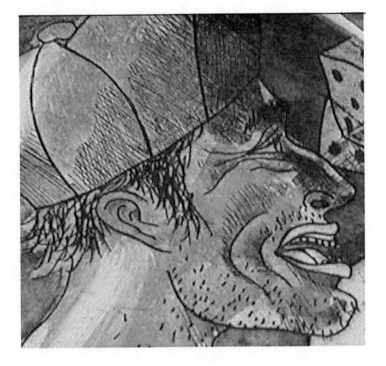